Beauty And The Beast
&
Sleeping Beauty

Beauty And The Beast & Sleeping Beauty

Fairytales Retold
Double Edition

Avril Sabine

Cracked Acorn Productions
Australia

Beauty And The Beast & Sleeping Beauty

Fairytales Retold Double Edition

Published by

Cracked Acorn Productions

PO Box 1365

Gympie, Queensland 4570

Australia

978-1-925131-79-6 (Large Type Print)

Genre: Fairytales Retold Short Story

Cover design by Caitlyn Petersen

Beauty And The Beast

*

Sleeping Beauty

Beauty And The Beast

Unable to believe her family's fortunes have changed, Belle asks her father to bring her a rose when he returns home. The rose brings more troubles to their family. The beast it belonged to demands either her father's life or one of his daughters. Belle can't let her father die, but she's terrified of facing the beast.

*

People have been telling stories since the beginning of time. Fairytales, folklore, myths and legends are among some of the stories that have been told over and over through the centuries. The basic story remains the same, but each storyteller adds their own style, sometimes adding something unique to the tale.

*

This story was written by an Australian author using Australian spelling.

Beauty And The Beast

Belle looked out the window again. Another day was nearly over and he hadn't returned. Snow had heralded winter's arrival and still her father wasn't home. Fear skittered through her, but she pushed it away. He was fine. Her brothers and sisters might have given up hope, but she hadn't.

The sound of footsteps had her hurriedly stepping away from the window. She could see by her oldest sister's expression that she hadn't moved quickly enough. Meeting

Annette's brown eyes, she said the first thing she could think of. "It's started snowing."

Annette shook her head, pity filling her eyes. "He's not coming. If he was he'd have been here by the end of summer."

Belle met Annette's dark brown eyes, which matched the colour of her hair. "No. He is coming."

Dion, the brother closest to Belle in age, entered the room in time to hear her words. He had the same brown eyes and hair as the rest of his siblings. "Let me go after him. I don't have to take the horse." Having only one horse had been the reason Annette had used last time she'd said no.

Annette turned towards him. "You can stop asking. No one is going after him. I'm not going to let anything happen to you or anyone else in our family."

Belle was torn between telling Dion he couldn't go, worried he wouldn't return, and telling Annette it was a safe journey. "Nothing has happened to our father. He's late. Only late." Belle pushed past her sister, not wanting to hear another word. She didn't walk away fast enough.

"He said he'd be gone weeks, not months."

She wanted to run back and tell Annette that meant nothing, but she knew it was pointless. Annette had already given up. Belle refused to accept that both their parents were gone. Her father had to come home. Stepping into the kitchen, she thought of the last time she'd seen him. He'd been grinning, his words tumbling over each other as he told them the good news. Joking with her brothers, teasing her sisters, asking everyone what they'd like him to bring home when he recovered their fortunes. She hadn't been able to believe the news could possibly be good. Not after everything that had happened.

If only she'd believed him. If only she'd been able to laugh and talk and make plans like the rest of her family. She remembered some of the superstitious sailors on her father's once numerous ships. One sailor in particular had believed bad luck could be brought along on a voyage by believing it would come with you. What if he'd been right?

Her father had to come home. She didn't want to be the one who'd brought bad luck to his venture.

Didn't want to be the one to make the good news, about one of his ships returning to safe harbour, to be false. After their house burned with all their possessions, then pirates had sunk her father's ships, she hadn't been able to believe. As each of their friends turned their backs on them, once they'd lost their wealth, she'd begun to expect only disasters.

When her father had asked her what she wanted him to bring home for her, she'd first asked for nothing, only his safe return. That hadn't stopped him. He'd continued to ask. And what had she asked for? A rose. A single rose that he could easily find in nearly any garden in town. A rose that most people would give him for the price of a thank you. She hadn't believed their fortunes were about to change.

The back door opened and two of her brothers entered, dragging her back to the present. Her oldest brother, Roland, carried a hare. Beside him, Hubert dusted snow from his clothes and shook it from his hat. He was a year younger than Annette, the third oldest of her siblings.

Roland dropped the hare onto the wooden table in the centre of the kitchen. "Looks like the snow has set in."

Belle couldn't help thinking about her father being caught out in this weather. Shoving that image from her mind, she pictured him instead by a warm fire in a tavern somewhere. Possibly talking to merchants about selling them the goods he was hoping to find on his ship that had returned.

Annette pushed Belle out of the

doorway to glare at her brothers, hands on her hips. "Who is going to clean up this mess? You've got puddles all over the floor and you haven't skinned the hare."

"Don't start. You try being out in the cold all day trying to catch something for dinner." Roland strode towards Annette, stoping in front of her, Hubert at his side. "Why don't you do it? Taking care of the house isn't anywhere near as hard as hunting and working the fields." Roland pushed past her.

"I haven't finished talking to you," Annette called after him before she turned to Belle. "You can skin the hare and clean up the puddles. Make yourself useful rather than moping around all day."

Annette left the room before Belle could argue. She glared after her sister for a moment before facing the kitchen. Her shoulders slumped. He had to be safe. All she wanted was for him to return home safely. She barely remembered what it was like to be rich. It had been over two years now. Having servants and fine clothes seemed like another lifetime. One that was almost a dream. She didn't need that life back. What she did need was her father home.

* * *

Belle sat by the fire, trying to concentrate on the mending spread out over her lap. Her needle stopped as her gaze darted towards the window. A glance towards Annette and Camille, one of her other sisters, showed their heads bent over their mending. That would change if she crossed the room to peer out the window again. She doubted Annette would believe she was any more interested in finding out how much snow had fallen than she'd been the last two times she'd tried that excuse.

How could they sit there so calmly? Didn't they want to look outside at every single sound? Her needle continued to remain still. Again her gaze was drawn to the window. Maybe they should let Dion travel the three hundred miles to the town, where they'd once lived, so he could see why their father was taking so long to return. She stared at Annette. Convincing her sister would probably be an almost impossible task. They had to do something. How could Annette expect them all to stay here and never even bother trying to find out where he was?

A noise outside caught Belle's

attention. She could sit still no longer. She was across the room and peering out the window before Annette could speak, the mending lying in a heap on the floor by her seat. She pressed a hand against the cold glass, her breath fogging up the window. She tried to speak, but it seemed such a complicated process. Again she tried. Giving up she raced for the front door, flinging it open. She ran outside, not bothering to stop and gather her threadbare shawl, ignoring Annette who called out after her.

The cold air bit into her flesh and seared her lungs, but she couldn't stop. She ran down the rutted road, laughing and crying, unable to look anywhere other than at the man riding towards her. When he dismounted she flung herself into his arms. Then her siblings were around them, all talking at once.

Aubin, her father, tightened his arms around her as she continued to cling to him, even while her sisters tried to do the same. He was home. He was alive and safe at home.

"This is stupidity, standing around out here in the cold," Annette said. "Come in and sit by the fire."

"Where did the horse come from?" Dion asked.

"And the fine cloak you're wearing." Roland rubbed the edge of the garment between his fingers.

"How much money did you make from selling the goods the ship brought back?" Hubert asked.

"Come sit by the fire, Father." Camille tugged on his hand.

Belle reluctantly let him go, clinging to his other hand, afraid to let him out of her sight. "What took you so long?"

Her father shook his head. "Nothing went as planned."

"But you made money, didn't you?" Josette, Belle's sister who was only a couple of years older than her, asked.

Belle held her breath, waiting for the answer. She knew how much losing everything had meant to Josette. Knew how devastated her sister had been when they'd lost their wealth and her fiancé's family had refused to allow her to marry their son.

"I need to stable the horse," Aubin said.

"I'll do it." Timothee, one of Belle's brothers, took the reins. He started to walk away, throwing over his shoulder, "Don't say anything until I'm back."

Belle remained at her father's side as Annette first settled him in his armchair by the fire, then sent Camille to make him a warm drink. The questions continued, but Aubin brushed them all aside. He patted the arm of the chair, tugging Belle closer.

She perched beside her father, drinking in the sight of him. He looked tired. There were shadows under his eyes and more grey in his dark brown hair. "What happened? Why were you gone so long?"

Aubin shook his head. "Not now." He drew a silk wrapped item from his belt pouch. Placing it on his lap, he slowly unwrapped it to reveal a perfect rose. He held it out to her. "I could not have imagined the cost when I picked this rose for you."

"What do you mean?" Annette demanded.

Again Aubin shook his head. "Later." His gaze was drawn to the fire. "I will tell you all later."

Timothee strode into the room. "I didn't miss anything did I?"

Aubin rose to his feet. "I will tell you after I wash and have something to eat. It's been a long journey."

"Was there anything on the ship to sell?" Josette wailed.

Aubin held her gaze a moment. "A better question would be, what other misfortunes have befallen us." He turned away, walking slowly from the room.

Josette burst into tears, flinging herself into the chair her father had vacated.

Belle stared at the empty doorway. Clasping her hands together, the stem of the rose caught tightly, she tried not to think of all the possible problems his venture might have brought upon them. What else could go wrong? They had no money left to lose, the once large fleet of ships were gone, their many friends treated them like they were diseased and all they owned was this one house, three hundred miles from the nearest town. Surely that wasn't it. Not their house. Where would they live if they lost this place too?

Her siblings left the room, one by one, until only Josette and Annette were left. Annette stared down at Josette, hands on her hips, slowly shaking her head. She turned to Belle. "Instead of standing around moping, you can help me with dinner." She strode from the room before Belle could argue.

With a last look at Josette, Belle wandered towards the kitchen where Annette was ordering Camille around. She held back a sigh when Annette noticed her and started giving her orders too.

It was well after dark before Aubin sat by the fire again and told his children about his journey. Belle sat on the sofa beside Josette, who occasionally sniffled. Dion was on the other side of her, sending a glare towards Josette each time she made a noise. Belle fiddled with the stem of the rose as she listened. Aubin talked about reaching town only to find out the ship's goods had been sold since everyone had believed him dead. Weeks of arguing hadn't helped and he'd barely managed to get enough money together to cover the cost of his journey. Unable to afford to stay in town any longer he'd been forced to leave by the very merchants he'd once considered his friends. Not far from town a storm had started, but he'd known there would be no welcome in town so he'd pressed on instead of turning back.

The snowstorm had grown worse and he'd become lost, fearing he'd never make it home. When night had fallen, he'd huddled by his horse, praying the howling wolves didn't find him. The arrival of morning hadn't helped and he'd had no idea which direction to travel in. Wandering aimlessly he'd stumbled upon a path. Not knowing what else to do, he'd followed it. The rough and slippery track had eventually become an avenue of trees that led to a castle.

Cold, hungry, exhausted and

having nowhere else to go, he'd made his way to the front door of the castle. It had seemed deserted. Everything was in perfect condition, but he didn't see a single soul. Finding a room with a lit fireplace, he'd sat on a couch to warm himself while he'd waited for the owners of the castle to return. He'd fallen asleep to be woken hours later to a meal set on a table beside him, even though he was still alone.

The next day, rested, well fed, but having found no one, he'd ventured outside. After wandering around for a while he found himself in a rose garden. Outside the castle grounds it had been snowing, but here it looked like a mild summer's day. Every single rose bush had been in full bloom. A rainbow of colours filled the garden.

When her father remained silent, Belle spoke. "Is that where you found my rose?"

Aubin stared at her for several minutes. Finally he nodded.

"What happened?" Dion asked.

"Where did you get the horse," Timothee asked.

Aubin slowly shook his head, not answering either of his sons. "I didn't know. I never would have stolen the rose if I'd known."

Belle wanted to ask what hadn't he known. The ability to speak seemed to have disappeared again. Her fingers tightened around the stem of the rose.

"What happened?" Dion asked once more, the words quieter this time.

Aubin dropped his head into his hands, covering his face. "I didn't know." He continued to shake his head.

Belle wanted to run from the room. She didn't want to hear one more piece of bad news. But she couldn't bring herself to leave. She remained pressed between Dion and Josette, who continued to sniffle.

Aubin raised his head and his gaze met Belle's. "I wasn't able to bring back a single item of what each of you had asked for. No dresses, no boots, not one jewel. Nothing. I was returning to you empty handed. With less coins in my pockets than I'd left with. When I saw all those roses, I thought here was something I could bring home. One item from that long list that I could get." He shook his head, falling silent again.

Seeing the horror in her father's eyes, Belle looked away. Her gaze was drawn to the rose. Each red petal was perfect. The stem unmarred even after all her toying with it.

"There was a beast." Aubin's words were soft. "He demanded my life. I pleaded with him. I begged him to let me return home."

Belle's gaze remained on the rose. She was unable to look away from each dark red, perfect petal.

"Eventually he told me that if I would give him one of my daughters he would spare my life. He gave me the cloak to keep me warm and the horse to take me home quickly."

The rose fell from her fingers, landing on the floor. Each petal still perfect. Around her the room erupted into arguments. Josette began to cry again. Some of her brothers offered to go fight the beast. Corinne, her third eldest sister, pointed at her and said it was all her fault.

"Quiet." Aubin slowly stood up and the room fell into silence. "I would have none of you sacrifice yourself for me. What kind of father do you take me for?" His gaze travelled the room, stopping on each of his children. "I have come home to bid you farewell. To tell you what has happened so you're not left to wonder. The beast gave me a month to return. That will be more than enough time to settle my affairs." He crossed the room, stopping in front of the sofa, holding out his hand. "Come Josette, enough tears."

Josette flung herself into his arms, her sobbing growing louder.

Looking up, Belle met her father's gaze. She saw the fear in his eyes, the slump of his shoulders. She forced herself to stand up, stepping on the rose that was still lying on the floor. Words caught in her throat. This was her fault. If only she'd believed him. If she'd only believed their fortunes were about to return, she would have asked for something else. She thought of the sailor. Thought of how she'd brought bad luck to her father's venture by not believing in him. Again she tried to speak. Nothing. She swallowed, fearing the tightness in her throat would grow worse until she was unable to breathe.

"I will go." Her voice sounded strange to her ears. No one paid her any attention. Josette continued to cry, her brothers plotted the death of the beast and Corinne blamed her over and over again. Corinne was right. This was her fault. She took a deeper breath, barely managing to get it past the tightness of her throat. "I will go." This time her words were loud enough to bring silence to the room.

Aubin let Josette go, reaching for Belle.

She stepped to the side. "I will go."

"I can't let you. What kind of father would I be to deliver you to a fearful beast?"

She tried not to think about that part of going. Tried to focus only on the fact that it was all her fault. She hadn't believed so she'd asked for a rose. "What kind of father would desert all his children for the sake of one?"

The room erupted into arguments again. Belle turned away. She headed for the bed she shared with two of her sisters, unable to listen anymore. If she did, she might give in to her father's arguments and let him go. How could she live with that guilt? How could she let her father die because she'd asked for a rose? Because she hadn't believed he could restore their fortunes.

* * *

It was a week before Aubin was resigned to Belle's determination to go. A week during which Belle avoided her family as much as possible. She couldn't risk one of them talking her out of her decision. Then it was another week before they were ready to go. So many times Belle wanted to tell her father she'd changed her mind. So many times she'd wanted to beg him to leave immediately so she didn't have the chance to change her mind. In the end, she remained silent, continuing to avoid her brothers and sisters.

It was Dion who cornered her the morning she was to leave. She had nothing to take, only the clothes she wore. Her few possessions remained on her bed, each with a scrap of paper with the name of one of her siblings. They'd need the items far more than she would. She had even worn her most threadbare dress, shivering slightly as she stood on the doorstep, pulling away from her brother's hand that rested on her shoulder.

"Don't do this."

"What would you have me do instead? Let our father die?"

Dion shook his head. "No. We should go after this beast. Father must be mistaken. No creature is invincible, no matter how ferocious they look."

She stepped away when Dion reached for her again. "I have to do this. Please stop trying to talk me out of it."

"You don't. There has to be something else we can do. Anything else."

She could hear the desperation in his words. "No." This time she let his hand fall on her shoulder.

His fingers tightened. "So we're meant to sit back and let you sacrifice yourself? Meant to wave you off and forget about you?"

"Will you forget me?"

"No. Never." He crushed her to him. "Don't do this."

She held onto her brother for a moment before she slowly drew away. "I was the one who asked for a rose. I could have asked for jewels or dresses like the rest of our sisters. But I didn't."

"Why didn't you?"

She remained silent a moment, meeting his gaze, seeing a mixture of fear and anger in them. "Because I didn't believe our fortunes had finally changed."

"You were right."

Belle shook her head. "No. I was wrong." She didn't explain her words before she turned away and started to head towards the stable where she was to meet her father.

"Belle."

She stopped, her back still to her brother, blinking furiously as she focused on her breathing. "What?"

"Come home if you can."

She held herself still a moment, her eyes momentarily closing. Then she nodded before forcing herself to stride towards the side of the house. The rest of her siblings were crowded around Aubin and she remained apart, unable to join them where they stood in front of the stable. Josette was crying again, her face red and blotchy from days of tears. Annette gave their father last minute orders, straightening his scarf before she turned away, freezing when her gaze fell on Belle.

Annette remained there for nearly a minute, the rest of her family slowly turning to see what had caught her attention. Silence fell. Annette straightened her shoulders, striding towards Belle. "Look at you. Do you want to freeze before you reach the beast?" She tugged off her own coat and helped Belle into it. Her fingers remained on the top buttons, her gaze focused on them. Then she threw her arms around her sister. "Oh Belle. Be careful. Maybe it won't be so bad."

Nodding, Belle drew away, unable to speak. The rest of her siblings followed Annette's example, hugging her tightly before letting her go. When the last of them had said goodbye she looked towards her father who was now mounted on the horse. Shaky steps brought her to Aubin and he swung her up behind him.

As they rode away, Belle looked over her shoulder, her gaze travelling from the cluster of her siblings waving, still in front of the stable, to the house where Dion stood silently by the front door. Unable to watch a second longer she faced forward, closing her eyes. The horse picked up speed and Belle clung to her father, her grip loosening when the gait of the horse remained smooth. Never before had she been on such a fast horse. She could only believe that the creature was magical with the impossible speed he kept up.

By early evening, they were riding between an avenue of trees. As they travelled through the trees coloured lights began to shine in all directions. Ahead she could see the castle. Fireworks filled the sky around it. The air grew warmer, like a mild summer night and instead of putting her at ease, it only made Belle fear the end of the journey even more. How had the beast known they'd arrived?

But more importantly, why was he celebrating? Surely he wasn't so hungry that her arrival could warrant such rejoicing. When the horse stopped, they dismounted and walked up a flight of steps leading to a terrace. She followed her father as he headed inside the castle, gazing around at the magnificent surroundings. It was far more impressive than the home they'd once lived in. She was surrounded by all kinds of precious goods. Gold, silver and jewels decorated many of the furnishings.

Aubin entered a room, gesturing towards the small table set with a meal for two, a chair for each of them. "This is the room I stayed in last time I was here."

"Where is everyone?" Belle sat at the table.

"I saw no one but the beast when I was here."

Belle had a mouthful of food, surprised she was able to eat. "Someone must have prepared this meal. And who keeps everything clean?" She knew how much work it took to keep a cottage in order. A castle would take an army of servants.

Aubin shrugged. "If there are servants, I saw none."

They fell silent as they finished their meal. When Belle was about to ask her father what they should do next, the sound of heavy footsteps sounded in the corridor outside the room. She rose to her feet, wrapping her arms around her waist as she stared at the door.

Aubin came to stand beside her, dropping his arm across her shoulders. "It's not too late to change your mind. I'll stay and you can return home."

The door swung open and anything Belle might have said remained unspoken as she stared at the large, shaggy beast that stood before her. She wanted to turn and run, but was frozen to the spot. When he stepped into the room, she wanted to shrink away from him. Instead she remained immobile, terror rooting her in place.

"Sir, I've brought my youngest daughter. Belle."

The beast came further into the room, stopping directly in front of her. "Did you come willingly? Was it your choice to remain instead of your father?"

His voice was a deep growl and the sound of it made Belle think of wild vicious creatures waiting to rip her apart. She couldn't stay. Yet she also couldn't bring herself to speak the words to tell him she wanted to go home.

"Belle?"

Threaded amongst the growl she

heard concern in his voice. Surprise had her raising her gaze to meet his soft brown eyes. Instead of the cruel gaze she'd expected, she found worry. What did such a large and strong creature have to fear? Her arms loosened their grip on her waist and fell to her sides. "Yes." The word was little more than a whisper and she didn't know if she replied to his question or answered because her name had been spoken.

The beast nodded. "That is good. I told Aubin he was only to bring one of his daughters if she was willing."

She was staying? Panic flared and Belle started to say he was mistaken. That she didn't really want to remain with him. Her father spoke before she could.

"Will I be able to return to see my daughter?"

"No!"

The growl rang out in the room and Belle trembled, wanting to run, but still unable to move. Her mouth opened several times without results. Her words had disappeared again.

"You will leave tomorrow. Do not rise from bed until you hear the bell ring. Then you can leave as soon as you have eaten your breakfast. You will find the same horse to take you home." The beast turned his gaze towards Belle. "Take your father into the next room and help him choose everything you think your brothers and sisters might like. There are two trunks for you to fill. Your family should have something precious as a reminder of what they gave up." The beast turned and strode from the room.

Belle stared after him, finally able

to move. She faced her father and was about to beg him to let her go home, but she saw the fear on his face as he stared at the empty doorway. Forcing herself to reach for his hand, she wrapped her fingers around his. "Come and have a look at what's in the room." Her voice was soft and hesitant. She took a deep breath, trying to focus on the warmth of her father's hand and his humanness. Thinking about the things that made him different from the beast. "Aren't you curious?" She was relieved to hear her voice sound more like her own.

"Are you certain you want to stay?" Aubin asked.

She couldn't answer him. Instead she tugged on his hand, taking a step towards the doorway. "You must be curious. Come and have a look with me." She managed a slight smile, taking another step towards the door.

"It doesn't feel right to leave you here." Aubin slowly walked beside Belle to the next room.

When she swung the door open, her gaze was first drawn to the two large trunks sitting open in the middle of the room. Then the riches displayed on the shelves, that stood beside cupboards, caught her attention. She hurried into the room, opening cupboard doors to see what was hidden behind them. Dresses fit for queens hung in rows, matching jewellery in other cupboards. Belle flung open every door, before she stopped in the middle of the room. Slowly turning, she tried to take in the wealth surrounding her.

"Are you sure you want to stay?"

Aubin continued to stand in the doorway.

Belle faced him, seeing the mix of amazement and worry in his eyes. What else could she do? Leave and deprive her siblings not only of their father, but an escape from poverty? She was the one who'd asked for the rose. She was the one who hadn't believed. It was her fault they were in this predicament. Nodding her head, she tried to smile. "How could I not want to stay in a place like this?" And yet she didn't. She would have preferred to return to the cottage they'd lived in for the past few years. Would rather toil from dawn till dusk. She held out her hand. "Help me choose presents for everyone."

Between the two of them they filled the trunks with all manner of treasures. Gold, jewels, fine clothes and ornaments. Once the trunks were filled, they strapped them shut, standing back to survey the room. It seemed like barely anything had been removed.

Aubin stepped forward and tried to shift one of the trunks. "The beast is tormenting us. All this wealth and it will be impossible for me to take it home."

Belle's heart sank. Then she remembered what had happened the last time she'd doubted. "Why don't we have a sleep and see what the beast has to say in the morning?"

It took Belle a bit of time to convince her father, but they eventually returned to the other room. There was a narrow bed for each of them and Belle curled up in the one furthest from the door. She thought she might have trouble falling asleep, but it seemed like she'd no sooner laid down before the sound of a bell woke her.

Sitting up, she saw breakfast set out on the table where their dinner had been the previous night. She joined her father at the table, but this time she could barely bring herself to eat anything. Shortly her father would leave and it was more than likely she'd never see him again. Never see any of her family ever again. She couldn't help thinking of Dion standing at the front of their cottage watching her leave. Asking her to return if she could.

Once they'd eaten breakfast, Belle walked silently beside Aubin as they headed for the courtyard. Like the previous night, the place was deserted. She dreaded to think what it would be like spending day after day alone.

In the courtyard were two identical horses. One was laden down with the trunks that Aubin hadn't been able to move the previous night and the other was saddled. Aubin stopped beside the horse with the trunks, running his hand over the timber.

"They look like the ones we packed, but surely it would be impossible for any horse to carry such weight."

Belle looked at each horse. "Maybe they're capable of more than going fast enough to almost be flying."

"Or the beast emptied the trunks," Aubin said.

Belle inspected the area, worried the beast might have heard him. "No, I don't think so." Or at least she hoped not. The horse beside her pawed at the ground. "You had better go. The beast said you were to leave straight after breakfast."

"Maybe I could come back and see you one day."

"No, please don't." She shivered as she recalled the beast's refusal the night before. She didn't want any of her family returning and risking his wrath. "Tell my brothers and sisters that I'm happy to stay here. That I'm surrounded by everything I could ever want." Everything but her family. She pushed that thought aside, forcing herself to smile. "Tell them I love them, but they aren't to worry about me."

Aubin crushed her to him. "I will tell them, but no matter what you say, we will worry for you." He drew away, staring at her for several minutes before he mounted the horse.

He was barely seated before the horse burst into a gallop, the other horse following behind.

Belle stared after him as he disappeared into the distance. It was all she could do to stop herself from running after her father. Fighting back tears, she hurried inside. Around her the empty rooms of the castle seemed to mock her sorrow with their silence. She tried to explore, but she didn't have the heart for it. Instead she returned to the room she'd spent the night in and curled up on the bed, wishing she was at home with her family.

She drifted off to sleep and dreamt she was walking beside a brook edged by trees. Feeling lost and alone and more homesick than ever, she followed it.

"Why do you look so sad?"

Belle spun to face a young man. He was tall and slim with dark hair and brown eyes. "Who are you?" She slowly shook her head, glad it was only a dream. "Well of course you're no one. How could you be? You're only a part of my dream."

"I'm the prince of all the land here about, as far as the eye can see and even beyond that."

Belle smiled. Obviously she was a lot more terrified of her situation than she'd thought if she was dreaming up a prince to rescue her. "What is your name, Prince?"

"Prince will do for now. Eventually you'll learn my name, but not yet. Will you tell me why you're so sad?"

She didn't want to ruin such a pleasant dream by talking about her situation. "I'm afraid it's not a very interesting story. Why don't you tell me why you're here in my dream?"

"It's the only way I can visit you as I am."

"Why would you want to visit me?"

"Because you're both beautiful and brave."

She shook her head, recalling how she'd frozen in front of the beast. "No. You're wrong."

The prince reached for her hand. "I'm not wrong. You are brave. Didn't you face the beast without running from him?"

"Yes, but–"

"I need you to be brave, Belle. I need you to set me free."

"Set you free?"

"Yes. Don't trust too much in what your eyes can see and please don't desert me."

She couldn't refuse his pleading. She had no idea how she could help him, but she couldn't bring herself to desert him, even if he was only a dream. "I won't."

With a smile, the prince let go of her hand and the scene faded around her, forming into a stately room.

A beautiful lady came towards her, smiling. "Belle, there's no need for sorrow. Don't let yourself be deceived by appearances and you'll have a far better life than the one you left behind."

"Who are you?"

The lady laughed. "A friend. Now remember, do not be deceived by appearances."

The room faded away and the rest of her dreams were disjointed and confusing. She woke to the sound of a clock calling her name. Staring at the clock sitting on the small, ornate table beside her bed, she realised it had called once for every hour. She'd slept through the morning. It was now midday. Rising from the bed, she saw a dress and toiletries laid out for her as well as a meal. As soon as she'd dressed and had eaten, she left her room. Wandering around the castle, peering into rooms, soon became boring. There was no one to talk to and loneliness made her think of home.

Her family would all be busy at this hour. Her sisters would be working in the house, talking with whoever they worked beside and her brothers would be out hunting. Here there was no one. Room after room, all devoid of people. She entered a room of mirrors and saw herself reflected back so many times that she felt surrounded. Coming further into the room, she noticed a bracelet caught on one of the many branches of the chandelier that hung down low from the ceiling.

Stretching, she tried to reach it and failed. Jumping, her fingers brushed against it. She jumped again and this time managed to unhook it so that it fell into her hand. The jewelled bracelet was heavy in her hand and she examined it, gasping when she saw the portrait in the middle. It was the prince who'd been in her dream. She ran a finger over the portrait. What did it mean?

Looking around, she saw only herself reflected back endlessly. Who was he? How was she meant to set him free? Was he a prisoner of the beast? If the beast held him prisoner how could she rescue him? The moment he spoke to her she froze. She couldn't rescue herself let alone the prince.

Sighing, she slipped the bracelet onto her wrist. He'd asked her not to desert him. She had no idea how she could rescue him, or even where he was. And what did it mean that she couldn't trust her eyes? If he'd wanted her to rescue him, why couldn't he have told her what to do? She wished she could return to sleep so that hopefully she'd see the prince again. But she wasn't even close to being tired. Next time he visited her dreams she'd have so many questions to ask him. The first one being how to help him.

Leaving the room, she continued to explore, hoping that somehow she'd find the prince locked up somewhere. She found no one, only a room full of portraits. Standing in front of the portrait of the prince, she stared at him. How could she help someone when she didn't even know where they were?

Reaching out, she ran her hand across the cheek of the life sized painting of the prince. "I don't know what you want me to do." Her words were a whisper, but they sounded loud in the silent castle. "Why couldn't you have told me what to do?"

She stared at him a moment longer before she turned away, trying to find her room. Along the way she found a library filled with more books than she could read in a lifetime and a room with every musical instrument imaginable. She couldn't resist playing some of them.

As the day grew late and the

shadows lengthened, flames sprang to life on candles. Belle stared at an unlit candle, waiting. The flame seemed to leap from the wick. Reaching out, she quickly ran her fingers through the flame, feeling the heat. It was real.

She eventually found her room. It took her a moment to realise it was the correct room as the two single beds had been replaced by one large bed. It was the table she recognised. She stared at it. There was another meal set out, this time for two. The beast had been the only one she'd seen in all her explorations. How was she meant to sit down to a meal with him?

Hearing his heavy footsteps in the corridor she hurried further into the room, turning to face the doorway. When he stepped into the room, she froze, unable to move.

"Good evening, Belle."

It took her several attempts before she could make herself speak. "Good evening, Beast."

The beast made a sound that might have been a laugh, but was more like a rumbling growl. "My name is Leon."

"I'm sorry."

He bared his teeth and gestured towards the table. "Take a seat. Dine with me."

She forced trembling legs to carry her to the table and sank onto the seat. She watched as the beast joined her, picking up the cutlery in his great paws. Trying to contain her surprise, she continued to watch as he cut up his food and ate it. He behaved like a man. Was that what the prince had meant? Not to be deceived by the beast's behaviour? That no matter how much he acted like a man, he would only ever be a beast.

Leon gestured towards her untouched meal. "Aren't you hungry?"

She picked up her cutlery. "A little." She'd been more than a little hungry until she'd realised the beast would join her.

"What did you do today?"

She shrugged, suddenly conscious of the bracelet she wore. "Explored. Played some instruments." She shrugged again, not sure what else to tell him.

"What did you find in your explorations?"

"The instruments." Should she mention the bracelet? Did she want him to realise she knew about the prince? What would the beast do to the prince if he learned he was trying to escape? She'd said she wouldn't desert the prince, but how could she face the beast if she angered him?

Leon stared at her for a moment. "Do you think you could be happy here, Belle?"

Again she worried about what she should say to him. What would he do if she angered him? "How could I not be? I'd be very hard to please if I couldn't be happy here."

The beast pushed his empty plate away from himself. "Do you love me, Belle? Will you marry me?"

She stared at him, momentarily speechless. How could he ask her such a question? "I don't know what to say."

"The truth. Don't fear to tell me the truth."

She hesitated, still not certain that was the best choice. She feared it might anger him if she said no. "I don't know you. How can I love someone I don't know?"

He rose from the table. "Goodnight then, Belle. Sweet dreams."

She watched as he strode from the room, wondering why she felt saddened by the sorrow she'd heard in his voice. Had he expected her to say yes? Surely not. He'd told her to tell the truth. That was all she'd done. Told the truth.

Not knowing what else to do, Belle began to get ready for bed. When she eventually lay down, sleep took ages to come.

Once asleep, she found herself by the brook again. Gazing around the area, she spotted the prince and hurried towards him. "Tell me how to help you. I have no idea how to help you escape."

The prince reached for her hands, taking hold of them. "What did you do today?"

"Please tell me how I can help you."

He slowly shook his head. "I wish I could, but I can't talk about it."

"What can you talk about?"

"Many things. Now tell me, what did you do today?"

She sighed, tugging her hands from his. How was she meant to help him if he didn't tell her what he needed help with? "Is it the beast?"

"Please, Belle. I really can't answer your questions. I need your help, but I can't tell you what you must do. Please don't desert me."

She heard anguish in his tone and wanted to comfort him. "I won't." She held his gaze a moment longer before her gaze was drawn to the bracelet she wore. "I found this." She raised a hand so he could see it.

"It pleases me to see you wear it. Come, walk with me." He held out a hand to her and she took it.

They walked beside the brook, talking and occasionally laughing. The first time she laughed, Belle was surprised. She'd thought she'd never be able to laugh again. But here, in her dreams, she'd found a friend to talk to. Someone to help keep the loneliness at bay.

The prince finally bid her farewell, fading from her dream. She reluctantly woke. Lying in bed, she stared at the ceiling. Maybe she was wrong. How was it possible to dream of a real person you'd never met before? Lifting her arm, she examined the portrait. It wasn't large enough to show her every detail so she could know for certain that the prince in her dreams was the same as the one in the portrait. Rising to her feet, she ignored the meal set out for her and hurried through the castle until she reached the portrait room. Standing in front of the painting of the prince, she stared up at him. It was the man from her dreams. The man who'd begged her to help him. If only she knew how.

After several minutes she sighed then returned to her room. She dressed for the day and ate the meal before continuing her explorations. Today she headed outside, wandering the pathways that twisted through the many gardens. She discovered an aviary and the birds there called out her name. She tried speaking to them, hoping they were as magical as some of the other things she'd found. All they did was repeat her name. Finding a small ornamental cage, she took several of the birds back to her room, hoping their cheerful sounds would make her feel less lonely.

Returning to the gardens she wandered further from the castle. She found the brook and stood beside it, gazing at the water. How could she have dreamt this place? Every little detail was the same. The only difference was that she was alone. She slowly turned, examining the area carefully. She was completely alone. The prince was nowhere to be seen. Where did the beast keep him? How could she possibly find him in a place as vast as this? It was impossible.

Shoulders slumping she meandered back to the castle, oblivious to her surroundings. In her room she found the midday meal on the table. She picked at the food, not very hungry after having discovered the brook.

She spent the afternoon continuing her search of the castle. The end of the day found her standing in front of the portrait of the prince. "I won't give up." She stared at him a moment longer before she returned to her room to find the table set for two.

The beast arrived not long after she had, gesturing for her to sit down. Belle sat, keeping a wary eye on the beast as she did so.

"Good evening, Belle."

This time the words came easier, although she did stumble over his name. "Good evening, Leon."

"What did you do today?"

She spoke about the birds, talked of the fountains in the gardens, the brook she had walked beside and the numerous rooms she'd discovered.

The beast told her some of the places she might like to look at the next day and Belle nodded, not certain what to say.

"Are you happy here, Belle?"

Meeting his gaze, she hesitated. He seemed so sincere, but the prince had warned her that appearances could be deceptive. "There's so much to see and do that I'd be very hard to please if I wasn't happy here."

"And are you?"

What could she say? Why did he have to insist on asking? "I miss my family. I've never been away from them before."

"Do you love me, Belle? Will you marry me?"

Like the night before, she hesitated, afraid of making him angry. "I still don't know you. I can't love someone I don't know."

The beast rose from his chair. "Goodnight, Belle. Sweet dreams."

She watched as he left the room. Did he know the prince visited her in her dreams? Was that why he said sweet dreams? She didn't know, but she had to be careful of what she said so the beast didn't learn the truth. Rising from her chair, she prepared for bed, hoping to see the prince.

* * *

Weeks passed and her life fell into a routine. During the day she explored the castle and its grounds and each night she dined with the beast. Afterwards he always asked her to marry him and every time she declined. While she slept, the prince visited her and they wandered about the grounds, talking and laughing. Occasionally the beautiful lady visited her and told her not to give up, not to desert the prince, but mostly it was the prince who kept her company in her dreams.

One evening, several months after she'd first arrived at the castle, she walked through a rose garden as she headed back towards the castle. She stopped to stare at the numerous flowers surrounding her. The scent of roses filled the warm air and she reached for one of them. Her hand fell away, leaving the rose still on the bush. She thought of her family. Her father, her sisters, her brothers. It had been days since she'd last thought of them. Days since she'd thought of anyone other than the prince and the beast. How long would it be before she forgot her past completely? She stood there, bringing to mind each of her family. The last to come to mind was Dion, standing at the front of the cottage, watching her leave. Were they all well? Had there been anything in the trunks? Or had the beast tricked them?

"What can I do to make you happy?"

Belle spun to face the beast. She'd been so caught up in her thoughts she hadn't heard him arrive. "I was admiring the roses."

He reached past her and picked one, holding it out to her.

She stared at the perfect, dark red petals thinking of the first rose she'd been given from these gardens. The rose her father had picked. She met his gaze, trying to read his expression. It was impossible. Taking the rose she breathed in the scent of it. "Thank you, Leon."

"What can I do to make you happy?"

To Belle, his words seemed like a plea. They made her want to reach out and comfort him. She hesitated then rested her hand on his arm. His hair felt soft beneath her palm. "I am happy. Most of the time. I was thinking of my family. I was wondering how they fared." She was surprised to realise that most of what she said was true. Most of the time she was happy here. And not just during her dreams she spent with the prince. There were so many fascinating areas to explore in and around the castle. Even the meals she ate with the beast were entertaining. She no longer feared he'd eat her, but she still worried at times about what might happen if she angered him. Would it be possible for a beast to control himself if he was angered beyond reason? She didn't know and preferred not to find out.

"I would like to let you visit them, but I fear you'd never return."

She started to argue that she would, then stopped. "I don't know either." She liked to think she wouldn't desert the prince, but she wasn't certain.

The beast held out his paw. "Will you dine with me?"

Removing her hand from his arm, she reached for his paw, still holding the rose he'd given her. "Yes, Leon."

Once the meal was over, the beast stared at her before asking his usual question. "Do you love me, Belle? Will you marry me?"

She held his gaze, surprised at how sad she felt that she couldn't give him the answer he wanted. "I'm sorry, Leon." She thought of the prince's warnings. She'd tried to remain wary of the beast, but it seemed she'd failed. "As much as I care for you, I don't love you."

The beast rose from his chair. "Goodnight, Belle. Sweet dreams."

"Sweet dreams, Leon."

He remained standing, staring down at her for several minutes. "Thank you. I will."

She continued to sit, staring at the empty doorway, unable to bring herself to move straight away. Tonight, instead of immediately retiring to bed she headed for the portrait room. She felt like she should be apologising. Reaching out, she rested her hand against the painting of the prince. "I haven't deserted you." She stood there a little longer before she retired for the night.

More months passed and Belle

began to look forward to not only her dreams, but also dining with Leon. Sometimes they walked through the gardens first and he showed her many of his favourite places. Soon she began to be as much at ease with Leon as she was with the prince.

One evening in the gardens, Belle asked, "Do the seasons never change here?"

"For as long as the castle remains under a terrible enchantment the seasons won't change."

"An enchantment?"

Leon reached out and ran the back of his paw against her cheek. "You seem much happier these days. Are you happy here, Belle?"

She took his great paw in both her hands and smiled. "Yes, Leon." When she looked at his face, she no longer saw a terrifying beast. She saw human eyes that stared back at her with so many different expressions. "Shall we dine?"

Leon nodded and led her to the dining room where they'd taken to eating for the past month.

That night, when the prince came to Belle in her sleep, he asked, "Do you no longer care for me?"

She threaded her fingers through his. "Of course I do."

"Then why have you forgotten my warning not to trust too much in what your eyes can see? I need you to set me free, Belle."

"I'm trying. Why can't you tell me what to do? I've searched everywhere for you. I haven't deserted you."

"Is that what you do with your days? Search for me?"

She could have said yes, but it

wasn't the complete truth. "Sometimes."

"What do you do the rest of the time?"

"I spend it with Leon."

"The beast?"

She nodded.

"Do you care more for this beast then you do for me?"

"I care for both of you."

"Don't you find him a terrible creature? Terrifying?"

"Maybe once, but not any more."

"And if you had to choose between us, who would you pick?"

She felt his fingers momentarily tighten on hers. Bringing to mind Leon, she tried to compare them. It was impossible. How could she choose between them? There were a surprising amount of similarities. Their humour, some of the topics they discussed and the way they treated her. "I don't know."

The prince smiled. "Then it's a good thing you don't need to choose." He paused. "Walk with me?"

When Belle nodded, the prince headed for the brook where they wandered for the rest of the night until she was woken in the morning by the clock.

* * *

The evening Belle realised she'd been at the castle for a year, she couldn't help making her way to the rose garden. She brushed her fingers over the velvety petals of one of the roses, wondering how her family were. It hardly seemed possible that she hadn't seen them for so long. There were days, often weeks, that passed without her thinking of them. It was there that Leon found her.

"Why are you so sad this evening?"

She turned to him with a smile, unable to push aside her sorrow. "It's been a year since I last saw my family."

"I thought you were happy here."

She reached for one of his paws. "Oh, I am. But I'd love to see my family. It's been so long since I've seen any of them. I can hardly believe it's been an entire year."

"I fear you wouldn't return if you left."

This time she didn't hesitate. "Give me two months with my family and I'll happily return."

"Do you promise? If I let you go to your family, would you promise to return exactly two months from now?"

"Yes."

"You wouldn't desert me? You'd come back?"

His words made her think of the prince. "I promise."

Leon nodded. "I'll think about it. Come and dine with me."

Once they'd eaten, Leon remained silently at the table, staring at her. "Are you certain you'd return if I let you visit your family?"

"Yes."

"Do you love me, Belle?"

Her gaze roamed his familiar features and she reached across the table, taking hold of one of his paws. "I don't think so." Although she wasn't so certain any more. If it weren't for the prince she would have said yes. For surely if she really loved Leon she wouldn't also have such strong feelings for the prince.

Leon remained silent a moment longer. "You may visit with your family."

"Thank you." She rose to her feet, coming around the table to throw her arms around him. "Thank you so very much."

"I can refuse you nothing, even if it would cost me my life."

"I'd never ask anything of you that would cost you your life." The thought of him dying made her heart ache.

Leon gave her a plain, gold ring. "There are four boxes in the room next to your bedroom that you can pack with things you'll need and presents for your family. When the two months are up, say goodbye to your family and when you've gone to bed turn this ring around on your finger and say, 'I wish to return to my beast'. Make certain you return here when the two months are over."

"Yes, I will. Thank you so much." She drew away from him. "You can't imagine how much this means to me. I've missed my family terribly."

Leon stepped away from the table. "I'll see you when you return."

As soon as he'd left, Belle hurried to the room. She filled the trunks with clothes to wear and presents for her family. Once the trunks were strapped shut she made her way to the portrait room to stare up at the prince. After several minutes of silence she spoke. "I will return. I won't desert you." She started to turn away, then faced the portrait again. "You or Leon."

She hurried to her room and crawled into bed, falling instantly asleep. The prince came to her in her dream and he seemed dejected.

"What's wrong?"

"How can you ask that when you're deserting me?"

"Never. I'm only going so I can assure my family that I'm safe and well. I will return. I promised Leon I'd only be gone two months."

"What would that matter to you? He's a beast. Do you really mean to keep your word to him?"

"Don't speak about him like that. He can't help the way he looks. There's nothing beastly about the way he behaves."

"You promise you're not deserting me?"

She had to assure him several more times that she'd return before he would believe her. When her dreams eventually faded, she opened her eyes to find herself in a strange place, the trunks neatly stacked along the wall of the bedroom. Climbing out of the bed she hesitantly opened the bedroom door and peered into a carpeted corridor. She had no idea where she was. Stepping out of the room, she examined her surroundings. Everything was of the finest materials.

She started down the corridor, freezing when she heard her father's voice drift up the staircase she walked past. She hesitantly started down the steps, flying down them when she heard her father laugh. A sound behind her drew her attention and she turned to see Dion step out of one of the downstairs rooms.

"Belle?"

Laughing, she launched herself at her brother. Tears mingled with her laughter as Dion called for the rest of their family. The following hour was filled with laughter, everyone talking at once and numerous questions. They spoke of people they wanted her to meet, things they wanted her to do with them and places they wanted to take her.

Over the next two months Belle was kept busy. Her sisters took her to the numerous entertainments they regularly attended and introduced her to all their friends. Belle soon became bored with the constant parties and entertainments. She started to miss Leon, the prince and the castle. Not once did she dream of the prince while she was visiting her family and when the last day arrived, she was almost relieved. Tomorrow she'd see Leon and in the night she'd dream of her prince.

When she tried to say goodbye to her family, they begged her for one more day. They eventually convinced her that a single day wouldn't matter. And each day she tried to say goodbye, her family begged her to stay a little longer since they didn't know if they'd ever get to see her again. Several weeks soon passed.

She didn't know how long she would have let her family convince her to stay if she hadn't dreamt she was back at the castle. She found herself wandering the empty rooms, looking for Leon. He was nowhere to be found. Running from room to room, calling his name, she was still unable to find him. Then she searched the grounds. She'd nearly given up hope of finding him when she stumbled across a shady path that led to a cave. Leon lay collapsed on the floor.

Belle raced to his side, crouching down to check him. "Leon?" She watched as his eyes opened for a few seconds, then closed again. "Please, Leon. Speak to me. What's wrong?"

His eyes opened again. "You deserted me. You left me to die." His eyes closed.

She shook him. "Leon, please. Don't leave me."

The beautiful woman appeared beside her. "You may still save him. Another day and it may have been too late. You should have kept your promise."

Belle woke from her dream with tears coursing down her cheeks. This time when she said goodbye to her family she didn't let them persuade her to stay another day. She had to return to Leon. Had to see if he was fine. She didn't know what she'd do if anything happened to him.

When she went to bed that night, she turned the ring on her finger. "I wish to return to my beast." Hoping it worked, she fell into a dreamless sleep to be woken by the sound of the clock calling her name. Relief rushed through her. The ring had worked, bringing her back to the bedroom at the castle.

All day she prowled the castle as she waited to dine with Leon. But he never arrived. Just like in her dream, she ran from room to room, calling him. He was nowhere to be found. Remembering her dream, she searched the grounds, eventually finding the shady path that led to the cave.

Inside the cave she found him,

collapsed on the ground, barely alive. She threw herself over him. "I'm so sorry. I didn't think a few extra days would matter. Why didn't you tell me? Please Leon, talk to me. Don't leave me." She brushed away the tears that stained her cheeks. "Please, Leon."

His eyes opened and he stared up at her. "You came back." His voice was weak.

"Yes. Yes, I did." She stroked his shaggy head. "I was so terrified when I saw you lying here. I thought you dead and it broke my heart."

He pressed his paw against her cheek. "Why would you cry for a beast like me?"

"Because I love you."

"How can that be possible?" His voice was a little stronger. "Look at me. How can you love a terrifying beast like me?"

She continued to stroke his head. "How could I not?"

He captured her hand. "Return to the castle. I'll join you soon."

"If you don't, I'll come looking for you again." She rose to her feet, staring down at him for a moment. "Don't take too long." With a watery smile, she turned away and hurried from the cave.

When Leon joined her in the dining room, where dinner was set out, he brought a rose with him. Baring his teeth, he held it out to her.

Smiling, she took it from him, thinking back to the day she'd asked her father for a rose, now grateful that she had. "Thank you." She placed it beside her plate as she sat at the table.

They spoke about the time they'd

been apart. Leon spoke of missing her, while Belle talked about her family. Eventually the meal was over and Leon stared silently at her.

Belle smiled at him, impatiently waiting for him to ask his usual question.

"Do you love me, Belle?"

She grinned. "Of course I do." He made the rumbling sound that she knew was laughter. She laughed with him, waiting for his final question.

"Will you marry me?"

"Absolutely. As soon as possible." At her words, a blaze of light drew her attention to the windows. Fireworks exploded across the night sky, spelling out the phrase, 'Long live the prince and his bride'. She turned back to Leon to ask him what was happening. Her mouth dropped open as she struggled to find words.

"Leon?" She frowned. "Prince?" The prince sat in the seat Leon had been in only seconds before.

He rose from the table and came to stand near her, taking her hand. "Prince Leon."

Standing up, she continued to stare at him, trying to figure out what was going on. "No wonder I couldn't choose between you."

Leon chuckled. "I'm glad."

The sound of a carriage arriving had them both peering out the window. They went down to greet the two women who stepped out of it. Belle recognised one of them from her dreams. Leon introduced her as a fairy and the other woman as his mother.

Leon's mother hugged her tightly. "Thank you. How can I ever repay you for breaking the terrible enchantment my son was under?"

Leon spoke before Belle had a chance. "By offering your consent and giving us your blessing. We're to be married as soon as possible."

"Of course I will," Leon's mother said.

"We'll arrange it immediately," the fairy said. "Do you want me to bring your father, brothers and sisters here so they can dance at your wedding?"

Belle nodded before she turned to Leon. "Are you sure this is what you want? You aren't marrying me just to break the enchantment, are you?"

Leon drew her to his side. "How could I not want to marry someone as brave and beautiful as you?"

She opened her mouth to argue that she wasn't brave. Before she had a chance to speak, his lips met hers and her argument was forgotten as she slid her arms around his neck. She would tell him later. Much later.

Sleeping Beauty

While searching for adventure, Prince Philip stumbles across a castle surrounded by an impenetrable thorny hedge. He learns it's the home of Briar Rose, a princess cursed to sleep for a hundred years. The curse can only be broken by true love's kiss. He fears it might be an impossible curse to break and yet he's compelled to attempt it anyway.

*

People have been telling stories since

the beginning of time. Fairytales, folklore, myths and legends are among some of the stories that have been told over and over through the centuries. The basic story remains the same, but each storyteller adds their own style, sometimes adding something unique to the tale.

*

This story was written by an Australian author using Australian spelling.

Sleeping Beauty

Prince Philip leaned low over the neck of his horse, urging him to go faster. He checked over his shoulder, trying to see through the closely packed trees. Had he lost them? He didn't know. His guards were persistent. Although he couldn't blame them. His father wouldn't be impressed if they allowed anything to happen to him.

Seeing an even narrower path off to his right, he took it, slowing down slightly when the branches grabbed at him. The path looked unused, grown over in some places. He remained leaning over his horse's neck, unable to sit up with how low some of the branches hung down. Again he glanced behind, hearing and seeing nothing. He slowed his horse to a walk. All he wanted was his chance to have an adventure. His father spoke of the adventures he'd experienced when he was eighteen. And yet his father continued to treat him like a child. He sighed heavily as he thought of the many times his mother had clung to both his hands and begged him not to go chasing after danger. Then reminded him of all the misfortunes that had befallen him as a child in his pursuit of adventure.

He wasn't a child and he was perfectly capable of looking after himself. If he could manage to lose his guards long enough to prove exactly how capable he was, then everyone else would realise it too. When the path narrowed even further, he dismounted from his horse, wondering if he should turn back. It looked like no one had travelled this path in decades. Whatever had once been at the end of it was probably long gone, fallen into ruins and reclaimed by the forest.

The end of the path came sooner than he expected and he stopped in a large cleared patch of ground staring at a thorny hedge that rose up in front of him. There was easily thirty feet between the densely growing trees at his back and the hedge in front of him. None of the trees grew any closer, ending abruptly as if someone or something kept them in check.

He tied the reins of his horse to a

narrow tree and stepped further into the clearing. Above the thick wall of thorns he glimpsed the towers of a castle, vines clinging to the stone walls. Leaving his horse, he walked around the outside, looking for a way through the thorns. After nearly ten minutes he began to think there might not be an entrance. Stopping, he looked back in the direction he'd come, his eye catching sight of something a gust of breeze caused to move deep within the hedge. He tried to push his way through the hedge, but the branches clung to him. Thorns scratched his hands and face as they tried to wrap around his arms and legs every time he moved. He froze when he realised what it was that had caught his attention. Held in place by large, sharp thorns was the skeletal remains of three heavily armoured knights.

The branches were twisted around their arms and legs like they were vines, the thorns pressed hard against bones. The hedge held them upright even though they were long dead. Their armour was rusting and the sword of one of the knights remained at the ready, thorns holding it in position. How had they died? Surely it wasn't the hedge, which was even now relaxing its grip so Philip could move forward. But he didn't. As much as he wanted to find a way to the castle, he began to think forcing his way through the hedge wasn't it. Turning, he tried to push his way out. Branches clung to him and thorns pressed against his skin, making it nearly impossible to escape their sharp grip. He wondered if he should use the dagger in his boot. Before he could decide he stumbled out of the thorny hedge and into the clearing.

Looking down, he saw his once fine garments were ripped and torn. He looked like he'd been in a fight yet all he'd encountered so far was an extremely tall hedge of thorns. Not much of an adventure. He trudged back to his horse wondering if his parents were correct. Was he ready for an adventure? He'd been bested by a hedge of thorns. Admittedly an extremely large one, but it was still only a hedge.

Reaching his horse, he took a set of clothes from his saddlebags and changed into them. Swinging into the saddle, he headed back the way he'd come and past the narrow path that had brought him into the clearing. He'd ridden for nearly an hour, catching glimpses of men long dead in the depths of the hedge, before he came across an overgrown paved road.

If it hadn't been for the different sound his horse's hooves made on the ground, he wouldn't have noticed since his attention had been taken up by the hedge. He saw patches of the road between weeds, fallen leaves and dirt. To his right the hedge was as impenetrable as ever. To his left there was a narrow gap between the trees. The once tidy avenue was filled with straggling saplings, half grown trees and shrubs. Looking in the direction of the hedge again, he was torn. Surely in that direction lay adventure. But it was impossible to reach.

Turning away from the hedge he nudged his horse onto the overgrown road. After several hours the forest thinned, giving way to farms. Spying an elderly man sitting on his porch, whittling away on a piece of wood, he rode towards him hoping he'd be able to direct him to somewhere he could stay for the evening. There was very little light left of the day and as much as he was interested in finding adventure he didn't think encountering those that roamed the roads after dark was the kind he'd enjoy.

Dismounting, he walked closer to the porch, stopping at the foot of the two wooden stairs. "Good afternoon, could you tell me where the nearest tavern is?"

"You won't make it before dark."

"Would you have somewhere I could water my horse, then?" If he was forced to make camp on the road he should at least see to the needs of his horse.

The man remained seated, barely glancing up from his whittling. "There's a trough out the back. We don't get many who've come down that road. Nothing out that way but Briar Rose. I guess you didn't come to see her as those that do never return."

Philip was tempted to ask what he meant, but decided to take care of his horse first. "Thank you." He gave the man a slight nod before he headed around the back. Spying the trough, he led his horse over to it and tied him to the post nearby. Once he'd loosened the girth, he gave his horse a couple of pats on the neck before he returned to the front of the house. "Do you mind if I sit with you while my horse has a rest?" And while he tried to decide where to stay for the night. He didn't relish the thought of camping on the road. Not without his entourage. He fleetingly wondered where his guards had ended up after he'd lost them in the forest. Had they returned to the rest of the people who'd been travelling with them? Having more than twenty people to see to his every need hadn't been his idea of setting out to find adventure. He might as well have remained at home.

The old man finally shrugged. "Makes no difference to me." He continued with his whittling, only a single glance in Philip's direction.

Philip sat down on the timber chair near the old man. "You mentioned the name Briar Rose earlier. Is that the name of the castle?"

The old man chuckled, finally looking away from his whittling. "So you have been to the castle. Did you get past the hedge?" His gaze rested on each of the scratches visible on Philip. He chuckled again. "You obviously had a go at it by the looks of things."

Philip shook his head. "It was impossible. There was a moment there I thought I'd have to use my dagger to escape."

The old man grinned, several teeth missing, others yellowed with age. "I'm going to guess you didn't do anything so foolish or you wouldn't be here."

"Foolish?"

The old man slowly shook his head. "Will you be like all the rest, lad? Asking many questions and never using any of the answers. Nameless lords and princes who all thought they'd be the one to wake her."

He started to ask the man what he meant by nameless, then realised he hadn't introduced himself. Leaning forward, he held out his hand. "I'm Philip."

"Jacob." The man grasped his hand, his grip firm. "So what are you then? A lord, a prince?"

Philip started to answer prince, then grinned. "An adventurer." Hopefully. Although with the way his luck was going, it didn't look very likely.

Jacob chuckled once again. "I don't think we've have one of them headed for the castle. Not as I can recollect. Probably everything else. Knights and lords, dukes and princes. I believe there's even been a couple of kings. But they were long before my time, back in my great grandfather's time."

"Why? What makes them all try to

get past the hedge? What's so special about the castle?"

"Well now, that's a tale that'd take more than a few minutes. Might even take the night. Are you sticking around that long, lad? I don't suppose you've got anywhere else you can go. Not this close to dark."

Philip didn't hesitate. It sounded like Jacob was about to tell him of an adventure. "Is there somewhere I can put my horse for the night?"

"There's a small paddock out the back. Past the trough. It has a lean-to. I had my old mare in it until she passed on last year. I thought of getting another, but I'm getting too old and my son brings me all I need when he visits each week or two. I've no need to go anywhere these days."

Philip rose to his feet. "I won't be long."

It didn't take him long to put his horse in the paddock and check the fence was in good order. There was a trough with clean water near the lean-to and after unsaddling his horse, he headed back to the porch carrying the saddle and saddlebags. Resting them against the front wall of the house he looked around for the old man. "Jacob?"

"Come inside, lad."

Taking the half a loaf of bread from his saddlebags, Philip stepped inside the cottage. The old man was throwing diced vegetables into a pot hanging over the fire in the fireplace. There was a square, wooden table with four chairs set in front of the fire and a freestanding shelf off to the left that held crockery. At the other end of the cottage was an open door leading into a room with two single beds, well worn blankets covering them.

Philip strode to the table, placing the loaf of bread on the clean surface. "Is there anything I can do to help?" Not that he knew much about cooking, but it had seemed right to offer.

Jacob shook his head. "It's all sorted." He gestured towards the table. "Take a seat and tell me where you're headed."

He wasn't sure what to tell Jacob since he didn't have a clue where he was going. Instead he talked about some of the areas he'd passed through and asked Jacob about the nearest town, which he soon learned consisted of a cluster of houses, a single shop and a tavern.

Once the meal was ready, Jacob joined him at the table and they ate in silence. Philip wondered if it would be rude to remind Jacob he was going to tell him about Briar Rose.

The meal was nearly ended when Jacob spoke. "You're a bit of a quiet one, aren't you?"

It was all he could do not to laugh. He'd been thinking something similar about the old man. "It seemed rude to pester you about Briar Rose while you were eating."

Jacob slowly nodded, his gaze firmly on Philip. "We'll sit on the porch once the meal is done. I'll have my pipe and you can ask me as many questions as you wish."

Philip nodded, trying not to hurry with his food. As soon as the meal was over, he helped Jacob tidy the kitchen before he sat beside him on the porch. He tried to remain still, but found himself shifting in his seat as he waited impatiently for Jacob to light his pipe.

"It would have been over a hundred years ago when the king and queen of hereabouts began to think they'd never have a child. They'd been married for years and years and yet the queen remained barren. One day she was wandering along the river's edge when she saw a little fish floundering on the bank. Taking pity on it, she slipped it back into the water. She watched for several minutes, hoping she'd been able to save it. Then its head emerged from the surface of the river and it spoke to her. 'I know of your sorrow', it told her. 'You shall have a daughter'. The fish sank beneath the surface of the water, swimming away." Jacob paused to draw on his pipe.

"The fish spoke?"

Jacob nodded. "Yes. It was back in the days when the land was filled with magic. All sorts of magical creatures lived in the area including fairies and dragons. Most of them are gone now. Or live far from the people who've hunted them, used them and stolen their homes."

"Are there any more dragons?" Now hunting a dragon, that'd be an adventure worth going on.

Jacob chuckled. "There are probably a few, but most have been hunted down by adventurers and knights trying to make a name for themselves."

"If we didn't hunt them they'd continue to kill people," Philip said.

"They only attack people that have moved into their hunting grounds. It's the nature of the beast to want to live."

Philip opened his mouth to argue then decided he probably should remind Jacob of the story he was telling before the man wanted to retire for the night. "Did the queen have her daughter?"

"Yes." Jacob nodded, drawing on his pipe again. "They called her Briar Rose."

"The one that's sleeping? How long has she been at the castle? Didn't you say this happened a hundred years ago? How did that happen? What can make someone sleep for a hundred years?" He had so many more questions he wanted to ask, but guessed he should give Jacob a chance to answer those ones first.

"The king and queen upset the wrong person. Or should I say the wrong fairy. They held a feast to celebrate the birth of their long awaited daughter. Now it's unclear whether they only invited twelve fairies because that's all they had gold place settings for at the table, or if they forgot the thirteenth fairy still existed. She was quite old and had become a recluse. But fairies, they pretty much live forever, at least compared to us humans, and she wasn't happy to be forgotten."

When Jacob fell silent again, slowly nodding his head as he drew on his pipe, Philip asked, "What did she do?"

"Eleven of the fairies had bestowed their gifts upon the princess when the thirteenth fairy burst into the castle. She laid a curse upon the poor innocent babe so Briar Rose would prick her finger on a spindle before the end of her sixteenth birthday and die."

"But didn't you say she's in an enchanted sleep?" When Jacob nodded, Philip asked, "Then how did she escape the curse?"

"There was still one more fairy. All twelve of them had hidden when the thirteenth fairy had arrived and they crept out of hiding when she left. The queen was inconsolable and the twelfth fairy said that although she couldn't end the curse, she could change it so that instead of dying Briar Rose would fall into an enchanted sleep. There she would remain for a hundred years, only woken by true love's kiss. Now the king he was determined the curse shouldn't come about and had every spindle in the kingdom destroyed. They were all heaped together and burned. The stories say the fire lasted a week, filling the sky with its glow."

"If all the spindles were burnt, how did she end up in an enchanted sleep?"

Jacob shook his head. "No one can escape a curse, no matter what they do. The king and queen were away and had planned to arrive back on the day of Briar Rose's birthday. Instead so many things went wrong and they arrived home late. Far too late. Some stories say the king had missed a spindle in one of the towers. Other stories tell how the thirteenth fairy brought a spindle into the castle and enticed Briar Rose to use it. It's so long ago now that the truth has long been forgotten. It doesn't really matter which one it was, for the king and queen arrived home to find their daughter in an enchanted sleep. They had her dressed in the finery she would have worn to celebrate her sixteenth birthday and placed her on her bed. And so the princess wouldn't be woken to find she had no family and her people were long gone, the twelve fairies placed the entire castle into an enchanted sleep."

"Did they cause the hedge to grow?" Philip asked.

"No. It wasn't them. It was the thirteenth fairy. When lords and knights started showing up, trying to wake her, she set creatures against them and eventually caused the thorny hedge to grow. It grabs hold of whoever tries to force their way in and if that person should harm it, then the hedge never lets them go. Not even when they die."

"Harm it?"

"Break it, cut it, burn it. If you harm it in any way it'll grab hold of you and never, ever let go. It'll hold on tight for an eternity. You can see all of them trapped in the hedge. Even those who were caught when the hedge first grew, the ones who are long since gone and only their armour and weapons remain. And there they'll remain until the enchantment is broken and the princess woken."

Philip thought of the men caught in the hedge and how it had loosened its grip on him when he'd frozen at his first glimpse of the skeletons. Could he use that as a way to reach the castle? Instead of forcing his way through, could he slowly sneak forward every time the thorns loosened their grip? What if he should accidentally break a branch? Would he then be trapped for an eternity? "If it's that simple, why do they harm the hedge?"

"Now that I couldn't tell you, lad. Those with the answers are all long dead. It's been a while since someone came through looking for Briar Rose. Last time I was a lad about your age, maybe a little older, and I sat where we are now and listened to my father tell the tale." Jacob gestured towards Philip's seat with his pipe. He slowly rose to his feet, groaning as he straightened. "Time for bed, lad. I'm getting too old to be up all night."

Philip nodded, rising to his feet. Before he retired for the night he checked on his horse. He returned to the house and crawled into the spare bed, lying awake listening to Jacob snore softly while he thought about Briar Rose. She was only two years younger than him. Had her parents tried to stop her from doing anything? Had her mother wrapped her arms around her and begged her to remain close where it was safe, like his had done? And how had any of it helped? Her parents had burnt every single spindle in the kingdom and still she'd ended up trapped in an enchanted sleep.

When he finally fell asleep, his dreams were a jumble of images. Thorny hedges that tightened around his limbs, a castle filled with people having fallen asleep in mid action, a blue eyed girl with long blond hair asking him if he'd come to rescue her and a fairy telling him it wasn't time yet. Nearly, but not quite yet. Another fairy told him he'd never make it through her hedge alive. Her crows would pick his bones clean before he could escape.

Feeling unrested, Philip woke to the sound of Jacob pottering around in the kitchen. Once again he offered to help Jacob prepare the meal. The old man shooed him outside to check on his horse. When he returned, breakfast was on the table. Sitting down, he breathed in the scent of the steaming bowls of porridge laced with honey.

"So lad, what do you plan to do? Are you going to brave the thorns and try to rescue Briar Rose?"

Philip thought of the young woman he'd seen in his dream. "What do the stories say she looked like? Do any of them mention how she looked?"

Jacob chuckled. "Why beautiful of course. Is there a single princess who isn't?"

Philip smiled. He doubted anyone would dare call a princess anything other than beautiful for fear of what her parents might do. "What do they say she looked like? What colour are her eyes, her hair?"

Jacob frowned, laying his spoon in his nearly empty bowl. Finally his frown cleared. "Her hair is paler than bales of straw and her eyes are as blue as a clear summer sky. Her skin is like the finest of porcelain and her lips like rose petals." Jacob chuckled. "The old tales are always full of flowery words when it comes to describing princesses. I would be surprised if she really was as pretty as all that."

Philip thought of the girl in his dream. Surely it was a coincidence. He smiled, pushing aside the unease he felt. "If they'd said she was a troll, who'd want to rescue her?"

Jacob chuckled again. "I'm sure there are quite a few landless knights and impoverished princes who'd rescue the ugliest of princesses if she also came with a castle."

Philip didn't doubt it. He nodded in agreement.

Once breakfast was over, he thanked Jacob for his hospitality and saddled his horse. He sat out the front for a moment looking first in the direction of the town and then towards the castle. It took him a few minutes to come to a decision and he turned his horse in the direction of the thorny hedge. Hours later, when he reached the hedge, he stared at it unable to stop thinking about his dream. Had he really dreamt of the princess? And what about the two fairies? He thought of the second one's threat, shuddering at the thought of crows picking the flesh from his bones. A glance around the area showed he was alone. Not a single bird or beast in sight and particularly no crows.

He continued to stare at the tangle of thorns. What would it be like to be trapped asleep for a hundred years? Give or take a few days. Did she dream? Or had time passed her and all her people by, so that when they were eventually woken it would feel like they had only barely gone to sleep? Dismounting, he strode towards the thorny hedge, peering into the shadows. He caught glimpses of knights who had believed they'd be the one to reach the princess and wake her from her enchanted sleep. Their bony remains proved them wrong.

Still holding the reins of his horse, he tried to push past the thorns. Surely someone had to be able to get through to her. The old man had said it must be a hundred years by now. And yet the thorns fought against him entering and scratched at his hands. He retreated. It wasn't like he had his entire wardrobe with him to be able to tear yet more garments on the thorns.

Mounting his horse, he rode around the thorny hedge, trying to see a way into the castle. When he once again reached the main entrance, well after lunch, he began to think the old man was right. There was no way into the castle. The princess was probably trapped forever. Although if she could only be woken by true love's kiss she wasn't about to meet him while she slumbered inside her thorny cage.

Feeling hungry, he dismounted, taking food from his saddlebags. He sat against a tree, facing the hedge.

He doubted he'd be able to avoid his entourage forever. Not if he continued to stay in this area. If he really wanted to have his own adventures, instead of listening to those of others, he should keep moving. As much as he told himself it was time to leave, he couldn't stop thinking about Briar Rose.

Still thinking of her, he fell asleep, tired from his restless night. He found himself walking through overgrown gardens, the sound of splashing water drawing him further into them. He stepped between two hedges, badly in need of trimming. Sitting on the edge of a fountain was the girl from last night's dream, trailing her fingers in the water. He took another step forward and dried leaves crunched beneath his boots. She turned to face him and he couldn't help thinking about Jacob's description of the princess. It perfectly matched the girl in front of him. A girl who looked like the one from his dream.

"Are you here to rescue me? That's what they usually say."

Philip took a couple of steps closer to her. He could now see small fish darting around her fingers where they trailed in the water. "Who are you?"

Smiling, she rose to her feet, shaking the water from her fingers. "Does that mean you're not here to rescue me? How strange. If you're not here to rescue me, then why are you here? Although really, the only thing I seem to be in need of rescuing from is boredom. And some of those who've said they were here to rescue me have only made that worse. I've been kind of glad they haven't returned."

"Are you… I mean, well…" Surely she couldn't be the princess. That wasn't possible.

She giggled, dropping into a curtsy. "Briar Rose. And you are?"

"Philip."

"Just plain old Philip? Not King Philip or Prince Philip or even Sir Philip?"

"Should I be?"

"I don't know. I've never had someone without a title try to rescue me before." She grinned. "Maybe this'll be better. At least you shouldn't be as pompous as King Henry was. Do you know he wouldn't sit over there with me." She gestured towards a rose arbour with a stone seat sprinkled with rose petals and dried leaves. "He said it would soil his garments. I never saw him again after that. Do you know him? Do you know what happened to him?"

He thought of all the skeletons surrounding the castle, caught in the thorny hedge. Obviously no one had told her. Should he? "I've never heard of him, I'm sorry."

"I saw you yesterday, didn't I? Just for a moment."

"I think so." He remembered her from his dream. How strange that she'd seen him too.

"You disappeared so quickly. That hasn't happened before. They usually stay a while and talk to me. Nor have any of them returned after the first visit. How is it you've managed to come back?"

He shrugged, still not certain what was going on. Maybe it was only a dream brought on by Jacob's tales, but it felt extremely real. "What do you do here, while you wait to be rescued?"

"I'm not exactly waiting. I mean, waiting implies sitting around doing nothing, doesn't it? And I don't know that I need rescuing. I think it's my people and my parents who need rescuing. They're the ones who are missing. Even all the horses are gone from the stable. Actually the entire castle is empty. I haven't even seen a mouse. Well that's not true, the place isn't completely empty. There are the fish of course, but they're rather boring."

"Where is everyone?"

She shrugged. "I don't know. I've looked absolutely everywhere. And it's taken me quite a while to search because I'll be in the middle of looking in another spot and the next minute I wake up in my bed and I don't even remember returning to it. When I wake up, there's always someone different visiting me. Although sometimes I wake up and it's like there's someone nearby, but I can't find them. I don't even catch a glimpse of them, like I did of you yesterday."

Philip was at a loss as to what to say to her. Did she sleep until her next rescuer arrived? And why did she only wake then? Did her rescuer need to be asleep for her to see them? He was pretty certain he was sleeping. "Do you remember how you came to be here?"

She shook her head. "Well, not exactly. I was using a spindle. I didn't know what it was at first. This lovely old lady asked for my help. It's my birthday," she frowned. "Or it was my birthday. I'm not sure how much time has passed. My parents were hours late so I was exploring some of the towers. I have no idea why. I've never ever felt the urge to explore them before and yet that day all I could think of was exploring the towers. It was extremely odd."

"And the old lady?"

"Oh yes, the old lady. She said her hands ached and she had this thread she needed to spin by the end of the day and would I help her? I had no idea what it was. And it didn't look all that easy to use. She told me it was simple and explained what I needed to do. I remember sitting down at it and pricking my finger, watching as a single drop of blood fell to the ground." She fell silent a moment. "The next thing I knew I was waking up in my bed and when I walked into the gardens a prince was asking me if I was Briar Rose. It was so many people ago that I've completely forgotten his name. Do you know how I ended up here?"

He opened his mouth to speak, but the scene faded around him and he woke to his horse's wet nose against his cheek. He pushed his horse's head away from him, biting back angry words. It wouldn't have been deliberate. Sighing, he rose to his feet and patted the neck of his horse before swinging into the saddle.

With one last look at the hedge and the castle towers he could see above it, Philip turned his horse towards the overgrown road. It was the perfect adventure and he was unable to go on it. Maybe Jacob would know of another adventure. One that wasn't impossible. But as hard as he tried, he couldn't stop thinking about the princess. Had he really visited her, or had it been a dream brought on from listening to Jacob's tale? It had felt so real. More real than any dream he'd ever had before, including the broken dreams he'd had last night.

Not knowing where else to go, he returned to Jacob's place. The man was sitting on his front porch, whittling again.

Seeing him, Jacob chuckled. "Have you been off to visit the princess, lad?"

Smiling, he nodded. "Do you mind if I stay the night?"

"Make yourself at home, although I dare say you'll be the one with the tale to tell tonight."

Philip settled his horse in the paddock out the back, unsaddling him. It wasn't until after dinner, and they were seated on the porch, that Jacob asked him about his day.

Philip shrugged. "The hedge was as solid as last time. I don't think there's any way through it."

"You were gone the entire day and that's all the tale you have? Not much of an adventurer, are you lad?"

"I fell asleep when I stopped to have something to eat. While I was asleep I had the strangest dream. It seemed so real."

"Well, lad? Don't keep me in suspense." Jacob drew on his pipe.

"I dreamt that I was talking to the princess." He shifted uncomfortably, wondering if he should have said anything at all.

Jacob leaned forward, his pipe resting on his knee. "And was she as beautiful as the old tales say?"

"It was only a dream, Jacob. Only

a dream." He couldn't stop thinking about the girl he'd spoken to. How could someone as vibrant as her be a dream? But he'd been asleep, how could she be anything else?

"There's magic there. Even as a young lad I felt it. So what was she like? The princess. Was she beautiful?"

Philip brought her image to mind. "She was sitting on the edge of a fountain, trailing her fingers in the water. When she looked up at me she had the bluest eyes and the fairest skin and her lips matched the petals on the roses not far from her." He thought about the way her lips had easily curved into a smile and the laughter in her eyes. "Yes Jacob, she was very beautiful." He thought of her question. How was he to rescue her? He didn't have a clue. If he forced his way through the hedge he'd die like all the others who'd tried. Then what would happen to her? Would she return to her enchanted sleep only to wake years later when the next prince came along with empty promises?

Jacob chuckled. "I knew it. I knew she wasn't one of those ones as ugly as a troll and considered only as beautiful as her castle."

Philip couldn't help smiling at the man's comment, slowly shaking his head. "No, she certainly isn't as ugly as a troll. In fact she's far from it."

The two of them fell silent. Jacob continued to puff on his pipe while Philip stared out into the night. Eventually the old man rose to his feet and said he was going to turn in. Philip thought he might as well go to bed too.

His dreams were as much of a jumble as they'd been the previous night. He saw a hedge surrounding him. One of the fairies, the one who'd told him her crows would pick his bones clean, smiled at him. It wasn't a joyous smile. It was one that sent shivers up his spine at the evil look in her eyes. Then Briar Rose was reaching out to him, calling his name. He hurried after her, but she disappeared and no matter where he looked, he couldn't find her. It seemed as if every direction he turned there was something blocking his way. The thorny hedge, a flock of crows, a slumbering beast hidden in dark shadows and the thirteenth fairy who'd laid the curse on Briar Rose.

He woke before Jacob and quietly went outside to stand on the front porch, staring in the direction of the castle. He could see the tips of its towers from here and wondered which tower was the one Briar Rose had found the spinning wheel in. Hearing a noise behind him, Philip went inside and found Jacob making breakfast.

When they were seated at the table eating their meal, Jacob asked, "What are you planning to do today, lad?"

Philip tried to say it was time for him to ride on, but he couldn't bring himself to speak the words. "I'll probably have a look at the hedge again."

"You be careful. Remember not to harm it or you'll be trapped in there forever."

Philip nodded, having another mouthful of his porridge. This morning it was sprinkled with cinnamon instead of honey. He should probably go into town and replenish Jacob's supplies. He didn't want the old man starving. Maybe he'd go there instead of the castle.

As soon as breakfast was over, Philip helped clean up before he went outside and saddled his horse. He looked in the direction of town, certain that was where he was headed for the day. Instead he found himself turning towards the castle. All through the hours it took to ride there he kept telling himself he should turn around, that there was nothing for him at the end of the overgrown road. He couldn't bring himself to do that. When he reached the clearing, he tied his horse to a tree and strode forward. He wrapped his hands around a branch between the thorns and felt it twist and turn trying to wrap itself around him.

"Briar Rose." Only silence greeted his call. He called out louder. "Briar Rose." Nothing. He was crazy. Surely the castle wasn't filled with an enchanted princess and her people. That was a tale for little children. Jacob was probably chuckling away at how gullible he was. Yet still he couldn't leave. He stared into the shadowy depths of the hedge, seeing the skeletal remains of those who'd failed. He took a step back. He didn't want to be a nameless and forgotten lord or prince, something that Jacob told the next traveller about.

He moved away from the hedge and sat down, his back against a tree. He made sure there was enough distance between him and his horse so he wouldn't be disturbed like yesterday. Closing his eyes, he tried to relax. Sleep didn't come. Giving up, he opened his eyes and stared at the hedge again. As restless as his night had been, it was too soon since waking for him to fall asleep. He listened to the sounds of the forest behind him. The insects, the rustle of animals, the call of birds. He frowned. The sounds were only behind him, there wasn't a single sound in front of him. The hedge was eerily silent.

Rising to his feet, Philip crossed the clearing to stand in front of the hedge, listening intently. Nothing. Complete silence. He reached out a hand, his fingers touching the gnarled wood of the hedge. He heard the creak and movement of the timber. That was all. It was the only sound in the entire hedge. He pulled his hand away before the thorns could grab hold of him. Maybe there was something in what the old man said.

The silence wasn't natural. He retreated to a tree and sat down again, leaning against the rough bark.

He closed his eyes and focused on his breathing, trying to fall asleep. His eyes flew open when he thought he heard his name called. He listened carefully. He was alone, other than his horse. There was no one around to call his name. Closing his eyes, several minutes passed before he heard his name called again. This time he rose to his feet and walked around, peering into the forest and walking several feet along the road. There was no one. He guessed he must have been hearing things. And no wonder with the unnerving silence of the hedge in front of him.

Returning to the tree, he sat down and made himself comfortable. It didn't help, he wasn't in the least bit tired. He moved away from the tree and lay down, staring up at a cloudless sky. It reminded him of Briar Rose's eyes. He closed his own eyes, trying to shut out the image. Tomorrow he'd go to town and replenish Jacob's supplies and the day after he'd leave. He couldn't continue to wander aimlessly around the hedge in the hope that somehow he'd find a way through. It was obvious by all the skeletons that there was none.

He guessed he must have drifted off to sleep because he found himself walking through an overgrown garden. Briar Rose ran towards him with a smile. He came to a halt, staring at her.

"I've been calling you for ages. What happened to you yesterday? Where did you go? We were talking and then you were gone. I hate how that happens. I thought that wouldn't happen with you since you didn't say you were here to rescue me and you'd returned."

He shook his head, not sure how to explain to her that all he'd done was wake up.

"Well, never mind. You're here now, which means you must be different from all the others."

He wanted to ask her if she knew about the curse, but looking into her eyes he couldn't find it in his heart to speak the words when he saw the joy in them. "What did you do while you waited for me to return?"

"I wandered around the gardens for a while, thinking you might have gotten lost in them. Then I went inside and looked through the castle for you. After a while I ended up in the library and spent some time reading. When I grew hungry I went to the kitchens and had something to eat. Next I ended up in the ballroom where I couldn't stop thinking about my last birthday. We had a ball in there to celebrate. I'm meant to have one for this birthday. For some reason I keep thinking it's meant to be today, but I'm sure I thought that yesterday too. Time has become so confusing lately. I know something is wrong. And I'm not just talking about how my parents and all our people are missing. It's frustrating not knowing."

He reached for her hand, holding it in both of his. As much as he didn't want to tell her, she deserved the truth. "I was told a tale by an old man called Jacob which brought me here to your castle. I've been trying to decide if I should tell you. I think it might help you make sense of the way time is so confusing for you. Except I'm not sure you'll want to hear the story."

"I'm not going to like it, am I?"

He continued to hold her hand as he shook his head. "No." His voice was soft. He almost hoped she'd tell him she didn't want to hear. He was already regretting saying anything.

She slid her hand out of his, taking hold of just one of his hands. "Come on."

He walked beside her through the garden, eventually entering the castle. She led him through corridors, up stairs, through numerous rooms, down hallways and eventually up a narrow stairwell that led to an old timber door. She let go of his hand to open it. He followed her in, his gaze drawn to the spinning wheel in the centre of the circular room. He turned to her, wondering why she'd brought him here.

"Nothing has made sense since the moment I entered this room. The first time, not today. I want to know what's happening." She held his gaze for a moment. "I need to know."

Philip crossed the room and stared at the sharp point of the spinning wheel. There was a dark stain on the tip that could have been blood. On the floor was a dark, rusty stain where a droplet had fallen. He turned to face her, trying to find the words to tell her about the curse. Jacob's words came to mind and he began the story with the king and queen who'd longed for a child and had spent many years barren.

Partway through the story Briar Rose sank down to the floor and

Philip joined her, sitting beside her. She listened as he retold Jacob's tale and then began to speak of his own quest for adventure. He told her how he'd stumbled upon the thorny hedge that protected her castle when he'd been escaping his guards. When he spoke about meeting her in his dreams and believing he was asleep, yet again, he watched her expression carefully. Seeing the sorrow in her eyes, he wanted to comfort her, but had no idea what to say.

Silence fell between them, eventually broken by Briar Rose. "Do you think you'll be able to break the curse?"

"I don't know."

"Why didn't anyone else tell me? Why did they only ever say they were here to rescue me?"

"I don't know." He struggled to

find something else to say. Something that would take the sorrow from her eyes. He couldn't tell her he'd rescue her. How could he promise something he might not be able to accomplish?

"Is there a way I can help? There must be some reason why I wake every time someone comes to rescue me."

"I-" The scene dissolved around him and he woke, finding a crow had landed on his leg, which was stretched out in front of him.

It squawked at him before flying off and landing in the hedge. It turned its head from side to side, as if eyeing him off. The hedge didn't try and grab it, remaining completely still. With another squawk it flew into the distance.

Seeing the crow reminded him of

the thirteenth fairy's threat. Had she sent the bird? Or was it a coincidence? He didn't know, but the day was growing late and he probably should return to Jacob's home. Rising to his feet he strode to his horse and, swinging up into the saddle, rode back to the old man's place.

Like the previous night, Philip told Jacob about his day as they sat on the porch after dinner. Jacob remained quiet throughout the tale, his pipe lying forgotten in his hand.

"It'd be her bird, all right. You want to be careful, lad. There's still powerful magic near that castle. Her magic. And she won't want you rescuing Briar Rose."

"But I don't have any idea of how to rescue her. It's impossible to get past the hedge." He couldn't keep the frustration from his voice.

"I'm sure you'll find a way, eventually." Jacob rose to his feet. "Tomorrow though. Figure it out tomorrow. I'm off to bed and you look like you could do with a good night sleep too."

Philip said goodnight to Jacob, but remained in the chair on the porch, staring out into the night. Something moved near the road and he rose to his feet, walking to the edge of the porch. It took flight and moonlight shone on glossy black feathers as a crow flew off into the night. Was it the same crow as earlier? He didn't know. Sighing heavily, he decided he might as well go to bed. It was all he could do for now. Maybe he'd come up with an idea in his sleep. Although he doubted it.

He tossed and turned all night. Several times he heard Briar Rose call him, but he didn't see her. Once again the thirteenth fairy threatened to set her crows upon him if he didn't leave. Another fairy also came, telling him not to give up. When he woke the next morning he was still tired and after having breakfast with Jacob, he decided to ride to town for supplies. He caught himself turning towards the castle and forced himself to turn his horse in the direction of the town instead.

He arrived not long before lunch and entered the single shop that was next door to the tavern. After gathering the essentials, and a bunch of carrots for his horse, he placed everything on the shopkeeper's counter and waited for him to tally up the bill. At the far end of the counter, three old men stood around gossiping. He nodded at them in greeting.

The oldest one gestured towards the scratches on his hands. "Looks like you've been trying to get into the sorcerer's castle."

One of his companions said, "How many times do I have to tell you? It's an evil witch trapped in there."

The first man said, "It's a sorcerer's castle. It's where they meet to practice their black magic."

The two of them argued for several minutes and Philip was about to turn away when the third man, who had remained silent until now, spoke. "You're both wrong. My great granny, who had it from her granny, said it was a princess enchanted by an evil fairy."

Philip leaned forward. "Do you

know how to break the enchantment?"

The man slowly shook his head. "I was only little. Great granny passed on while I was quite young so I don't remember half the tale." He shot a look at his companions. "But it was a princess, not a sorcerer and not a witch."

An argument started between the three men and Philip was relieved when the shopkeeper told him the total of his bill. He handed over the coins, collected the supplies and headed outside to his horse. With some effort he managed to fit everything in the saddlebags and headed back to Jacob's. Even though it was late afternoon, and he had no hope of returning before dark, he couldn't stop himself from heading towards the castle the moment he'd left the supplies with Jacob.

Halfway there, he tried to convince himself to turn back. Even though it was dark, he couldn't bring himself to turn his horse around. He should be leaving the area before his entourage found him. He shied away from that thought. It wasn't something he could bring himself to do. Nor could he forget the sound of Briar Rose calling his name in his dreams last night. Or the threat of the thirteenth fairy.

He remained on his horse, staring at the hedge of thorns. If he left, would Briar Rose remain awake until he died? Or would she return to her dreamless sleep once he was no longer in the area? His gaze was drawn to the castle towers and he noticed a light flickering in the windows of one of them, smoke rising into the night to be lost in the dark. Panic raced through him. How was he meant to get in there? Was she safe? Would her and all her people burn if the place was on fire?

He had to get in there. He needed to save her. Dismounting, he tied his horse to a tree and then eyed the hedge. It seemed less dense near the ground so he lay down in front of it and tried to wriggle in. It didn't help. The branches curved down and caught him, holding him in place. He relaxed, waiting for them to loosen their grip so he could move forward again. It was taking too long. What if the entire castle burned before he reached her? Obviously not the outer walls as they were made of stone, but the inside where Briar Rose was. He wriggled forward a little more and then stopped as he waited for the thorns to let go of him.

He guessed he must have fallen asleep as he found himself lying in front of the fountain. Scrambling to his feet, he saw there was still smoke rising from the tower. He ran towards the castle, stumbling into things and wishing it was a full moon so he had more light to find his way. Grabbing a lit lamp from the foyer, he ran through corridors, up stairs, through rooms and backtracked several times as he tried to find the tower.

When he burst into the tower room, it was to find Briar Rose swinging an axe at the spinning wheel. It had already been half chopped up and in the middle of the room was a fire where she was burning the broken pieces of timber.

He leaned against the door relieved the castle wasn't burning.

"What woke you yesterday?" The head of the axe rested on the floor and Briar Rose leaned against the handle, facing him.

"A crow. Are you fine? I saw the smoke while I was awake."

She smiled. "Really? Do you think that means something? Maybe this," she gestured towards the burning spinning wheel, "will break the enchantment."

He pushed away from the wall, placing his lamp next to the one already sitting on the floor near the door. He came further into the room, holding out his hand. "Let me help you with that."

She shook her head. "No, I want to get rid of it. I didn't do anything wrong to her. Why curse me because of something my parents did?" She turned away from him and lifted the axe, swinging it at the spinning wheel. "It's not fair. She didn't have to do this to me. I was only a baby. It wasn't my fault she wasn't invited to the celebration of my birth."

A piece of the spinning wheel spun across the floor and landed at his feet. He picked it up and threw it into the fire. The flames leapt up before they settled down again. He watched Briar Rose as she continued to break the spinning wheel, her hair flying around her as she attacked it. When she eventually finished smashing the spinning wheel into pieces, Philip helped her slowly add the bits of timber to the fire. They stood side by side watching the flames devour the broken spinning wheel, the axe leaning against the wall behind them near the lamps.

As the last of the timber was devoured, the smoke rising from it turned a murky dark blue before it drifted out the window with the rest of the smoke. "That didn't look good," Philip said.

Briar Rose lifted her chin and squared her shoulders. "I don't care. I'm glad it's gone."

When a crow landed on the window ledge screeching loudly, both of them jumped back, bumping into the axe. It clattered to the floor. Philip recovered first, moving forward to chase the crow away. "Go on. Get out of here." He waved his hands at the crow.

The crow rose up from the window ledge, but remained.

Squawking and scolding, it's black eyes never left them.

"I'll get rid of him." Briar Rose came forward with the axe. Before she had a chance to swing it, the crow gave one more squawk and flew off. She leaned the axe against the wall near the window, rubbing her arms. "How can this be a dream? It feels too real to be a dream. Do arms ache when you dream?" She lifted her hair off the back of her neck and let it fall again. "Do you get hot from working in your dreams? There has to be some other explanation. This can't be a dream."

Philip stared at her, wishing he could offer a different explanation. "I was in the town today buying supplies for Jacob. There were three old men and when they heard I'd been here, they began arguing about the castle."

"About my castle? What did they argue about?"

Philip nodded. "Yes, your castle." He hesitated, trying to find the right words. "One said it's where sorcerers meet and another said an evil witch was trapped here."

"And the third?"

"The third said pretty much the same as Jacob." Philip held her gaze, wishing he could have told her something different.

"You're the only one who's talked to me. They told me who they were, where they'd come from and that they were going to rescue me, but never have any of them talked to me and told me the truth. They didn't seem interested in anything I had to say." She crossed the distance between them so they stood only inches apart. "What made you tell me the truth?"

He reached out and brushed a strand of fair hair back from her face. Before he could say anything, the crow flew in at them, attacking. Philip struck out at the crow with his hands. The sharp beak and claws drew blood.

Briar Rose raced for the door. "Philip." She half closed the door.

Still trying to protect himself from the crow, he dashed for the door and Briar Rose slammed it shut once he'd slipped through. He couldn't see her in the darkness of the stairwell, but at least the crow was on the other side of the door.

"Are you hurt?" Briar Rose pressed her hands against his chest.

He took hold of her hand, trying

to ignore the sting as her skin came into contact with his wounds. "A few scratches. Nothing more."

"Come to the kitchen and I'll clean them for you."

They made their way carefully down the stairs, collecting the first lit lamp they came to in one of the corridors. When they reached the kitchen, Briar Rose cleaned the blood from both their hands. Once she'd finished cleaning his wounds, she continued to stare at his hands.

"What's wrong?" He wrapped his fingers around hers.

"Is this possible in a dream? Surely a dream can't draw blood."

"It's an enchanted sleep. Maybe more things are possible in an enchanted sleep."

"Then where are my parents and

my people? Weren't they put into an enchanted sleep too?"

"I don't know." He opened his mouth to reassure her, when the scene dissolved around him. It was pitch black and he was lying in the dirt under the hedge and a crow was making a racket nearby. His hands clenched into fists as anger and frustration filled him. Wriggling back out of the hedge, stopping frequently to wait for it to let him go so he could move again, he rose to his feet, looking around for the crow. It was gone.

He found his horse still tied to a tree and swinging into the saddle, he headed back to Jacob's. Not wanting to disturb the old man when he arrived, he put his horse in the paddock out the back and nodded off in one of the chairs on the porch.

Jacob found him there the next morning and invited him in for breakfast.

When he washed the dirt from his hands, before he joined Jacob at the table, he saw there were new wounds. They weren't from the thorns. He stared at the marks the crow had made. Surely this was proof that whatever it was, it was more than a dream.

Even though he told himself he shouldn't, he found himself returning to the castle after breakfast. Over and over that week, he continued to do the same. His nights were spent with Jacob and his days were spent sleeping near the castle while he wandered throughout it with Briar Rose. The only thing that changed was the number of crows pestering them. They could now no longer venture into the castle gardens and Briar Rose had to keep every window in the castle closed. Philip had spent an entire visit running through the castle with her chasing out the crows.

It was now the start of the second week and Philip was still staying at Jacob's. He sat down at the table with Jacob for the evening meal, picking at the food he didn't feel like eating. All he could think about was how many hours it was until dawn and he could return to the castle and Briar Rose.

Jacob eyed him up and down. "Are you well, lad?"

"I'm fine."

"Are you sure? I hear you pacing on the porch some nights long after I've gone to bed."

Philip shrugged. "I sleep most of the morning when I visit Briar Rose." It sounded better than telling Jacob his dreams kept him from having a decent night's sleep. Now they were mostly filled with crows and the thirteenth fairy's threats.

"How restful a sleep can it be when you're wandering around in someone's enchantment?"

"I'm fine, Jacob. Don't worry about me. I'll sleep tonight since I didn't get to spend as much time with Briar Rose this morning." He'd been woken far too soon by a flock of crows.

"You be careful, lad. That fairy isn't one to be messed with." Jacob returned to eating his food.

That night, once Jacob was snoring softly beside him, Philip gave up trying to sleep and headed to the porch where he found himself pacing back and forth. Seeing there was enough moonlight, he saddled his horse, returning to the castle. He stared up at it silhouetted against the night sky, catching a glimpse of a light shining in the window of one of the upper rooms through the top branches of the hedge. He found a comfortable spot amongst the trees and tried to fall asleep. It took far longer than he liked, but eventually he was waking up on the castle doorstep and hurrying inside before the crows could find him.

Taking a lit lamp from the foyer, he wandered through the castle trying to find the room he'd seen the light in. He eventually found it and saw Briar Rose curled up in a chair, a book on the floor at her feet. He crossed the room and kneeled in front of her, reaching out to take her hands.

Her eyes slowly opened and she

smiled at him. "What are you doing here during the night?"

"I couldn't sleep."

Briar Rose laughed. "You couldn't? Then how are you here now?"

He rose to his feet, stepping back as she did the same. "Well, I'm asleep now, but I couldn't sleep before. I can hear you calling me in my dreams. I can't see you though, not unless I'm close to the castle when I fall asleep. Why do you call me? Is something wrong?"

"It's because I think I catch a glimpse of you so I call out to you, but then you're gone."

"I don't see you in my dreams while I'm at Jacob's. I did a couple of times at the start, but not anymore. Now all I see is the thirteenth fairy and her crows." He tried not to think about her many threats.

Briar Rose stared silently at him for a moment. "Do you think we'll ever be able to break the enchantment? How long can you continue to visit me in your dreams? What if one time when you fall asleep you can't find your way here? Will that mean I'm no longer awake? Or whatever this is called. I want my life back, Philip. How do I get my life back?"

"Briar…" His voice trailed off as he tried to think of something to say. Then he smiled at her, reaching out to cup her cheek. He knew he wouldn't be able to leave. It shouldn't have taken him this long to realise he couldn't imagine life without her. "I won't give up. Somehow I'll find a way to break the enchantment. Even if I stop being able to find you in my dreams, I won't give up. No matter how long it takes we will eventually break the curse." He lowered his head, his lips nearly touching hers.

A flock of crows attacked his sleeping body, dragging him away from Briar Rose. He jumped to his feet, drawing his sword to swing at them. "No! Go away. Leave me alone." He continued to yell at the crows who darted in and out, pecking at him, narrowly avoiding his blade.

When they flew away, he leaned against a tree, sheathing his sword and slumping to the ground, cursing the thirteenth fairy and her crows. Light was starting to fill the sky and he rose to his feet, slipping further into the forest, still staying within sight of the hedge. He had to return to sleep. Briar Rose needed him.

It took him more than an hour before he fell asleep again. This time he found himself in the ballroom. He had no idea where she was. "Briar Rose!" He flung the door open and stepped into a dim corridor.

"Philip." She ran towards him, grinning. Reaching him, she threw her arms around him. "What happened?" She brushed a hand across his cheek. "You're bleeding."

"It was the crows." They were definitely getting worse. Somehow they'd have to do something about them. He just wasn't certain what.

"Are you safe? Will they be able to get you while you're here with me?"

"I moved further into the forest."

"We need to do something about them."

Philip laughed. "I was just thinking that. Although we're probably better off doing something to break the enchantment first. Hopefully that will get rid of the crows too."

"I don't know how you're going to get past the hedge, not with all you've said about it." She sighed heavily. "It sounds impossible."

"No, it can't be. One of the other fairies told me not to give up so there must be a way. We just haven't figured it out." He continued to hold onto her, her arms wrapped around him. "We will figure it out. Somehow."

"What if you set the hedge on fire?"

He started to nod, then remembered Jacob's warning. "No, Jacob specifically said not to burn it."

Briar Rose opened her mouth to speak. Instead she remained silent, her eyes widening and her mouth remaining open as she looked past Philip.

He turned to see what had caught her attention. A large beast stalked towards them down the corridor. As soon as it realised they were both staring at it, the beast began to run towards them. Drawing his sword, Philip grabbed hold of Briar Rose's hand and pulled her into the ballroom. He slammed the door shut and the beast ran into it a moment later, making it shudder. Philip slowly backed away from the door, his gaze remaining on it as he continued to hold tightly onto Briar Rose's hand.

"What was that?" Briar Rose demanded. "Did she send it? The fairy?"

"I don't know. I've never seen anything like it before." He glanced around the room. "Is there another way out of here?" The door shuddered as the beast barrelled into it.

"Only into the gardens with the crows."

There was a cracking sound and the door burst open. "I'm not sure which is worse. This beast or the crows." Letting go of Briar Rose's hand, he stepped in front of her holding his sword up. "Run. I'll keep him busy."

"No, I won't leave you."

The beast growled and lowered his head.

"Go. Please Briar, go. I'll follow." The beast started to run towards them and Philip widened his stance. "Please."

"What about-"

He never got to hear the end of her sentence. He was jolted awake by people calling his name. It took him a moment to realise it was his entourage and they were coming closer. He scrambled to his feet, desperate to get back to Briar Rose. He couldn't leave her to face the beast alone. Sheathing his sword, he ran towards the hedge, lying on the dirt to try and wriggle underneath it. The branches curved down to wrap around his arms, the thorns digging in. He froze.

"Let me go. Let me go to her." They ignored his whispered pleas, taking their time to relax their grip. As soon as they had, he crawled forward as fast as he could before he was once again trapped. He made slow progress, hearing his people coming closer.

One of them finally shouted, "There he is. Crawling through the hedge." There were more shouts as they tried to get through the hedge to him and it grabbed hold of them.

"Don't harm it or it'll never let you go. If you stay still it'll relax again," Philip called out as he wriggled further forward, the hedge seeming to be uninterested in him with the crowd trying to push their way through. If only he'd known sooner that all he'd needed was twenty other people trying to force their way through as he tried to ease his way through the hedge.

"Prince Philip. Stop. Come back."

He ignored one of his guards who called out to him and continued to make his way through the hedge, pausing when necessary. Then he was through, having only taken fifteen minutes to cross what should have taken him a day if his previous progress was any indication. He scrambled to his feet, brushing off the dirt and leaves as he ran towards the castle. Crows flew at him from every direction and he protected his face as he continued to run forward. Reaching the castle he slipped inside, slamming the door shut. The crows beat against the door with their wings and pecked with their beaks, screeching out in anger at his escape.

Philip ran to the ballroom, passing people who'd fallen asleep in mid action. He burst through the door and came to a skidding stop. She wasn't in here. There were several maids who'd fallen asleep at their tasks, put into an enchanted sleep after Briar Rose had been trapped in hers. Apart from that the room was empty.

He ran through corridors calling her name, trying to find her. Was she still trapped somewhere with that beast? He flung open doors, peering into rooms and continuing to ignore the many people slumbering throughout the castle. He was only interested in finding one person. Fear kept him running and filled his voice as he continued to call for her. Where was she? He even checked the tower and saw only a pile of ashes in the middle of the room where the spinning wheel had once been.

He paused in the doorway, trying to think where he hadn't looked. Trying to think past the panic and fear. An image of her curled up in a chair, with a book on the floor at her feet, came to mind. Her room. He hadn't searched her room yet. He tried to think how to reach it. Several times he had to retrace his steps, but eventually he stood in her doorway, relief nearly making him weak when he saw her sleeping in her bed.

He couldn't take his gaze from her as he crossed the room. She seemed so peaceful, her fair hair spread out on the pillow around her. He sat on the edge of the bed, taking one of her hands. "Briar Rose." Her name was a whisper as he stared down at her. Leaning forward, he pressed his lips to hers.

Her eyes opened and she reached for him, her arms going around him. "Philip. I thought he'd get me when you disappeared."

Sitting back, he tugged her to him, his arms tightening around her. "I was terrified he would too." He smiled. "You're awake. This isn't a dream."

"It's not?" She stared at him a moment before she returned his smile. "It's broken? The curse is broken?"

"Yes."

"And my people?"

"I don't know." He helped her from the bed, not letting go of her hand. "Why don't we have a look?"

They stepped into the corridor, freezing at a menacing growl. Philip backed into the room, pushing Briar Rose behind him as he drew his sword. The beast stalked forward.

"As soon as the doorway is clear you need to run," Philip said.

"No." Briar Rose ran to the fireplace and grabbed the poker. She turned to face the beast. "She's done enough to me. To us. No more. I didn't deserve anything she did."

Philip nodded, attacking the beast as it leapt towards him. Briar Rose fought beside him, stabbing at the beast with the poker. The beast snapped and snarled, fighting ferociously, but they eventually ended its life. Looking up, Philip saw people crowding around Briar Rose's doorway. He slid his arm around her waist as several of them entered the room.

"Prince Philip? Prince Philip." A man pushed his way through the crowd, coming into the bedroom. "Are you unharmed, my lord?"

Briar Rose turned to Philip. "An adventurer?" She grinned.

He chuckled. "Yes, but I'm also a prince."

She laughed, throwing her arms around him. "So you're not completely different from all the other ones. You do have a title."

"I'm nothing like the others. They didn't realise who they were meant to be rescuing."

Briar Rose continued to hold onto

him, ignoring her parents who burst into the room, demanding what was happening. "And who were they meant to be rescuing?"

"Themselves." His lips met Briar Rose's. The king roared, demanding he unhand the princess while his own people started to tell the king about Jacob who'd told their prince about an adventure. He was pretty certain his people were wrong. He hadn't completed his adventure. It was only beginning.

Free Ebook

Subscribe to Avril's newsletter and receive a free ebook. This ebook is exclusive to those on her mailing list. To find out more about this offer visit:

www.avrilsabine.com/free-ebook

*

We value your privacy and will not sell, rent, exchange or loan your email address to third parties. Your information is confidential and you are under no obligation to remain on the mailing list and can unsubscribe at any time.

To The Reader

If you enjoyed this book, why not consider leaving a review to help other readers discover it too? Reader engagement is one of the few ways that lets an author know readers want more books in a particular series or genre. So leave a review and tell friends, not only about this book but also about other ones you've enjoyed, so you can continue to enjoy books by your favourite authors for years to come.

Dreams are meant to be lived,

Avril.

About The Author

Avril is an Australian author who lives with her family on acreage in South East Queensland. She writes mostly young adult and children's speculative fiction, but has been known to dabble in other genres. You can find more information about her at www.avrilsabine.com where you can also subscribe to her newsletter to be kept informed about new releases, current projects, blog posts and exclusive news.

Titles By Avril Sabine

Stories about strong characters and characters who discover their strengths.

SERIES

Assassins Of The Dead- Young Adult Fantasy/Paranormal

Book 1: Dark Blade

Book 2: Dragon Touched

Book 3: Society Against Vampires

Book 4: King's Request

Dragon Blood- Young Adult Urban Fantasy (with elements of romance)

(5 book series)

Book 1: Pliethin

Book 2: Wyvern

Book 3: Surety

Book 4: Knight

Book 5: Mage

Dragon Mage- Young Adult Urban Fantasy (with elements of romance)

(Series two of Dragon Blood series)

Book 1: Promise

Dragon Blood Chronicles- Young Adult Urban Fantasy (with elements of romance)

(Companion stand alone series to Dragon Blood)

Book 1: Oath

Book 2: Betrayed

Guardians Of The Round Table- Young Adult Fantasy LitRPG

(Co-written with Storm and Rhys Petersen)

Book 1: Dexterity Fail

Book 2: Goblin Boots

Book 3: Singed Feathers

Book 4: Frog Mage

Book 5: Crystal Mine

Book 6: Cursed Harp

Book 7: Treasure Seeker

Rosie's Rangers- Young Adult Western Steampunk

(6 book series)

Book 1: Justice

Book 2: Vengeance

Book 3: Treachery

Book 4: Accused

Book 5: Wanted

Book 6: Corruption

Mark Of Kings- Children's Fantasy

(Upper middle grade/preteen)

(4 book series)

Book 1: The Arena

Book 2: The Island

Book 3: The Assassin

Book 4: The King

STAND ALONE SERIES

Demon Hunters- Young Adult Urban Fantasy/Horror (with elements of romance)

Book 1: Blood Sacrifice

Book 2: Retribution

Book 3: Tainted

Book 4: Premonition

Book 5: Cursed

Book 6: Feud

Book 7: Extrication

Plea Of The Damned- Young Adult Urban Fantasy/Paranormal

(6 book series)

Book 1: Forgive Me Lucy

Book 2: Forgive Me Aiden

Book 3: Forgive Me Jena

Book 4: Forgive Me Kobe

Book 5: Forgive Me Marti

Book 6: Forgive Me Dawson

Realms Of The Fae- Young Adult Urban Fantasy (with elements of romance)

The Sword (short story in Like A Girl Anthology)

Heart Of Stone

Book 1: A Debt Owed

Book 2: Marked By The Hunt

Book 3: The Magic Collector

Book 4: An Unexpected Betrayal

Book 5: Imprisoned By Iron

Fairytales Retold (Short Stories)

Snow-White And Rose-Red

The Twelve Brothers

The Light Princess

Beauty And The Beast

Sleeping Beauty

Aschenputtel

The Golden Bird

The Frog Prince

The Death Of Koshchei The Deathless

Myths And Legends Retold (Short Stories)

Ion, Son Of Apollo

Sir Gawain And The Maid With The Narrow Sleeves

Princess Ilse, The Giant's Daughter

YOUNG ADULT NOVELS

Young Adult Fantasy (with elements of romance)

Elf Sight

Earth Bound

Young Adult Urban Fantasy

Stone Warrior (with elements of romance)

The Jungle Inside

Young Adult Contemporary (with elements of romance)

Through Your Eyes

The Ugly Stepsister

Perfect Little Princess

Young Adult Contemporary/ Paranormal

Whispers In The Dark (with elements of romance and same sex relationships)

Over Too Soon (with elements of romance)

Young Adult Sci-Fi

Experiment X-One-Six (Urban Sci-Fi/Superheroes)

An Endless Dawn (Post Apocalyptic Sci-Fi)

CHILDREN'S BOOKS

Dragon Lord (Preteen/early teens) (Fantasy)

The Irish Wizard (Upper middle grade) (Urban Fantasy)

SHORT STORIES

Urban Fantasy

Eternally Late

Dealings With Joe

Glimpses (short story in That
Moment When Anthology)

Contemporary

The Brat Next Door

Fantasy LitRPG

(Set in the same world as Guardians
Of The Round Table Series)

Tales Of Inadon 1: The Disc (Co-written with Storm and Rhys Petersen) (short story in Game On! Anthology)

Post Apocalyptic Sci-Fi

Compulsive Directive

NONFICTION

A Year Of Weekly Writing Exercises (Creative Writing)

Cooking For Families With Allergies (Cooking) (Co-written with Storm Petersen)

Tell Me A Story, Grandma (Memoir)

For the most up to date details on available titles visit:

www.avrilsabine.com/books/ bibliography

Disclaimer

This is a work of fiction. Names, characters, businesses, places, events and incidents are either the products of the author's imagination or used in a fictitious manner. Any resemblance to actual persons, living or dead, or actual events is purely coincidental. The opinions expressed or beliefs held are those of the characters and should not be assumed to be the opinions or beliefs of the author.